She crouched behind him, unable to stop the thought her patient's physique was a prime example of why a female shouldn't be a doctor, according to her last professor. *Oh, yes—we wouldn't be able to treat men without thinking of marriage. Ha!* She shook her head to banish the thought, now supplanted by admiration for the curve of his buttocks, and stood up. Put on her professional tone. Looked into eyes the color of a storm-brewing sky, and felt a rush of desire to run her hands through the shaggy blond hair.

Never. Never ever.

She breathed out, pulled herself back to the moment. "You're covered in glass."

"What else is new?"

"Are you in pain?"

"Some. It can wait. Not enough to concern me."

"You're going to have to take off your pants and lie on your stomach so I can examine you."

He didn't take his eyes off her as he said, "Well, then you're going to have to help. My hands…" He held out his hands, palms up, for her to see.

She realized he was right but resented her own huff of annoyance as he lifted his arms away from his sides. She reached for the buckle on his gun belt first, her irritation with his smirk making her proceed faster than she might have, with less care.

He grimaced.

"Did that hurt?"

"'Course it dang well hurt. I've got glass—"

"I can see you're covered in glass, Mister…?" It suddenly struck her she'd been so stunned by her patient she hadn't even got his name.

"Coltrane. Shiloh Coltrane."

Praise for Andrea Downing and...

ALWAYS ON MY MIND:

"This book was such an enjoyable read. I really liked how the story starts off... As you turn the pages of each chapter, the anticipation rises as you wait for Cassie and Coop to find each other again. There's a good supporting cast, providing an additional layer of enjoyment... Drama and packed with emotion, I highly recommend this book."

~Still Moments Magazine (5 Stars)

~*~

DEAREST DARLING:

"A page turning mail order bride tale that doesn't really follow the standard formula. Instead, the plot is fresh."

~Brenda Casto, Readers' Favorite, (5 Stars)

~*~

LOVELAND:

"A fantastical frontier epic! The author does such an incredible job of immersing the reader in the old west that they can nearly feel the grit of the dust on their face..."

~Sandy Ponton, InD'tale

Shot
Through the Heart

by

Andrea Downing

This is a work of fiction. Names, characters, places, and incidents are either the product of the author's imagination or are used fictitiously, and any resemblance to actual persons living or dead, business establishments, events, or locales, is entirely coincidental.

Shot Through the Heart

Cover Art by *Debbie Taylor*

The Wild Rose Press, Inc.
PO Box 708
Adams Basin, NY 14410-0708
Visit us at www.thewildrosepress.com

Publishing History
First Cactus Rose Edition, 2020
Trade Paperback ISBN 978-1-5092-3234-5
Digital ISBN 978-1-5092-3235-2

Published in the United States of America

Acknowledgments

My thanks to Patti Sherry-Crews, whose friendship and positive attitude is always a source of encouragement to this author.

My love and thanks to my daughter, Cristal Downing, who somehow manages to consider and comment on her mother's western romances while having far weightier concerns on her mind at the UN.

And my especial thanks to my editor, Nan Swanson. This book was actually edited during a time when the world was in turmoil and depression was laying its heavy hand on many a soft shoulder, including my own. Correspondence with Nan always seemed to lighten that touch, while her keen eye certainly made this a better book through which to escape the tribulations of a pandemic.

Part One — Chapter One

The first thing Shiloh Coltrane thought, as he went flying through the glass of the Painted Lady Saloon, was he was going to hurt like hell if he didn't first bleed to death. The second thought that passed through his slightly foggy brain as he hit the iron bar that served to protect the glass from kicking horse hooves, not flying people, was this was going to cost him big-time and rile every man in town. And as he landed on the wooden boardwalk, rolling away from the possibility of further infliction from the tied horses, glass shattering and splintering around him, the vision that had descended the steps from the second floor flashed through his mind's eye as if death was approaching and his entire life had come to this point.

Which in some vague way he was aware it had.

That woman. Soiled dove? Surely not. Too neat, prim, and fully clothed. So what was she doing there?

He lay for a moment as the boardwalk vibrated with a power not unlike an earthquake, and voices grew like thunder moving in. A slight odor of manure wafting up, the prickle and sting of fractured glass, and a knowledge that any which way he moved, pain was inevitable—all became apparent.

Then, as the repetitive squeak of the saloon doors invaded his hearing, Bozy the bartender's voice slammed into his brain: "That there glass come all the way from Pittsburgh, Coltrane. You know how much that gonna cost to replace? You know how I'm gonna have to cover up that there winda while we wait for a replacement? And the painting to be done? You know how much all that gonna cost? You! It's gonna cost *you*!"

Shiloh felt the scrape of the glass fragments as he lifted his head gingerly and twisted to look Bozy in the eye. He'd removed his gloves earlier, and in order to push himself up, with the tenderness of bruises just now becoming evident, he knew he'd have to risk some of those splinters embedding themselves further into his skin. He pivoted onto his buttocks, now conscious something had stuck him in the behind, right through his jeans and union suit. He pulled his legs in, bent, and somehow managed to squat, leaning forward away from his spurs. His hands found and gripped the window's iron bar behind him, and he pushed himself to his full height.

"You tell Ike to pay for that, Bozy. And tell him not to show his face in town or he'll have two windows to pay for."

"Ike's not gonna pay nothing. He ain't got two nickels to rub together. He's already hightailed it outta here."

"I see. So just because I have a ranch that actually sees a profit I'm supposed to pay on behalf of the dumb brute that just flung me through your window? Good luck with that." He glanced around for his hat and spotted it clutched in the hands of one of the soiled doves.

Without meeting his gaze, she held it out. Shiloh took it and nodded his thanks, dusted it down, more to see if he could get some glass splinters out of his hands than to get dust off the hat. He studied Bozy's face, a mix of upset and anger, worry and thought.

"I'll see what I can do about Ike." Shiloh tried to keep his voice noncommittal.

"You gonna shoot him?"

"No, I'm not gonna shoot him. Damn fool." His hands inadvertently slipped to his thighs but the discomfort stopped him from actually feeling for his Colts.

"Why'd you start that fight, then? You gotta chip on your shoulder big as all outdoors."

"I didn't start the fight. And I said I'd see what could be done."

"You're good with your hands, Coltrane. Usually. You can do the work."

"I guess. Maybe. Let me know when the glass arrives."

"Well, what the hell happened there anyway?"

The crowd drew a little closer, and suddenly Shiloh felt the air sucked from his lungs. He wanted to get out, get home, get the glass picked out.

"I asked him where Parmeter was."

It was as if the ring of onlookers moved as one person and took two steps back.

"Parmeter?"

"Yeah. You remember Parmeter? My sister's husband?"

"You been askin' 'bout Parmeter ever since you come back. Give it up, why don't you?"

A chatter punctuated by snorts and sly looks met this statement.

"I'm not giving up 'til I find out who killed my

sister and where Parmeter's gone. And I hadn't asked Ike before."

Bozy shook his head. "Looks like he don't know nothing 'bout Parmeter, from where I stand." He seemed to think a moment. "You best be gettin' on over to that new doc's."

"What new doc's? Since when do we have a doctor?"

Bozy's mouth puckered and moved like he didn't want to swallow something awful. "A few weeks back. Only temporary I'd think. Lives up near the fort, treats the Indians at the agency, comes down here once a week. Sees folks over in the storeroom of the mercantile. Name's Sydney Cantrell."

Shiloh eyed the mess of glass.

"You better get on over before Doc leaves. We'll clean up this mess, Coltrane, but you better be prepared to pay for it all. That's all I got to say."

Shiloh glanced around once more. The shattered glass at his feet caught the last of the sun's rays and sparkled like a field of diamonds. His boots would protect his feet from damage, but it was still unpleasant to walk over the particles, a crunch every step he took. And he ached like hell. Plus, he hoped whatever was sticking in his backside would come off with his jeans, but he sure felt sore as he limped across the road to the store.

The bell tinkled as he opened the door, and about seven heads turned toward him. All men. They sat on barrels, perched on boxes, leaned against shelves of tools and clothes. One was propped up on the main counter, peering through the glass at an array of jars of candy.

"You all waiting for the doc?" He was getting a headache, and the thought of a long stay wasn't appealing.

A mix of nods and yeses greeted the question as a woman, whose rotund belly bespoke her condition, came out the back door from the storeroom. The men all craned their necks as if trying to see behind the door, but no one else appeared. The woman just said, "Next!" as she departed, and the first of the men went in.

Shiloh's increasing pain and blossoming exhaustion, both of which faced a long ride home, made him think perhaps he could handle matters himself, or his ranch hand Bones could, but the man who'd gone in wasn't long. He sloped out the door and twisted his hat in his hand as if the good doctor had reprimanded him rather than treated his ill. He bobbed his head at the next patient and left.

And so it went, all fairly brief consultations with only two men coming out with medicine bottles, serious looks on their faces. The cowboy before Shiloh held the door for him, a look of disappointment on his face.

"Dr. Cantrell's pretty stern. You better be ill," he said.

"What?" Shiloh felt his brows meet as he peered inside the storeroom. "Holy cow," he mumbled. "Holy cow."

His vision from the saloon. Brown-gold hair with lights of red, a color he couldn't remember ever having seen before, and blue eyes like a Wyoming sky, almost violet. Her skin was pale, pure and unblemished, like satin he imagined. He was tongue-tied.

Dr. Cantrell had her arms crossed against her chest as if she were protecting herself, but she breathed out a weary sigh. She studied his face.

"I'm Sydney Cantrell," she murmured at last. "Looks like you're lucky not to have lost your eye."

"My eye?" He started to bring his hand up but noticed he was dripping blood from a cut.

"You better sit down. If you can."

He looked around, and there was one wooden chair that looked as if it had been brought in from someone's dining room, the shopkeeper's most like, and a sturdy long table, which may have served as a dining table once. Her doctor's bag sat in a corner, open with several medicines and whatnot sticking out. He started to lower himself onto the chair but let out a yelp that would have awakened the dead.

"Here." She took his arm and guided him to the table. "Let me see."

Embarrassed in a way he'd never thought possible, he stood to consider whether to make a dash for the door and deal with things himself.

"Look," he said. "I think I better go. I thought…"

"You thought I was a male doctor. Everyone does."

"Until they see you."

"Hang your hat on the back of that chair and let me get to work."

She crouched behind him, unable to stop the thought her patient's physique was a prime example of why a female shouldn't be a doctor, according to her last professor. *Oh, yes—we wouldn't be able to treat men without thinking of marriage. Ha!* She shook her head to banish the thought, now supplanted by admiration for the curve of his buttocks, and stood up. Put on her professional tone. Looked into eyes the color of a storm-brewing sky, and felt a rush of desire to run her hands through the shaggy blond hair.

Never. Never ever.

She breathed out, pulled herself back to the moment. "You're covered in glass."

"What else is new?"

"Are you in pain?"

"Some. It can wait. Not enough to concern me."

"You're going to have to take off your pants and lie on your stomach so I can examine you."

He didn't take his eyes off her as he said, "Well, then you're going to have to help. My hands..." He held out his hands, palms up, for her to see.

She realized he was right but resented her own huff of annoyance as he lifted his arms away from his sides. She reached for the buckle on his gun belt first, her irritation with his smirk making her proceed faster than she might have, with less care.

He grimaced.

"Did that hurt?"

"'Course it dang well hurt. I've got glass—"

"I can see you're covered in glass, Mister...?" It suddenly struck her she'd been so stunned by her patient she hadn't even got his name.

"Coltrane. Shiloh Coltrane."

She pulled herself together once more as she stood, disconcerted, her gaze avoiding his. "Perhaps you'd like to see the barber? This is something he can—"

"If I wanted a shave, I'd see the barber. What I want is...what I want is to get this dang glass out of my skin, my hands particularly. And the piece that's sticking me in the...the...behind."

"There are bits in your face, as well." She reached for his belt without another word and undid it, hanging

Andrea Downing

the gun belt on the chair before reaching for his pants belt and pulling it free. That, too, landed on the chair.

"I know I've got bits in my face. Let's just deal first with the hands and…and behind."

"All right," she said. "I'm not going to take your pants off for you. Let me see your hands."

Once more, Shiloh held out both hands, palms up.

Flustered, she blurted, "Sit down." She went to her bag and searched for the carbolic, gave it a shake before putting some on a cloth and wiping a pair of tweezers. She pulled a tin basin out of the bag, too. She pivoted back to find him still standing. "Sorry, I forgot. You can't sit, can you?"

"Not really. Am I causing you problems?"

"No. But it's late in the day and I have a ways to get back. I've had a stream of cowboys in here who wanted nothing more than to ogle me, a few men throwing insults at a woman who thinks she can be a doctor, and the day is catching up with me. Give me your right hand first. You are right-handed, I take it."

"Yup."

"Fine." In the dim light of the storeroom, brightened only by a single window at a time of day with fading light, she bent over her patient's palm and began to pick out what she could see of the glass fragments, dropping each into the basin placed on the floor. After a few moments, she straightened herself and reached around with her free hand to rub her back.

"Maybe it'd be better if I held my hand higher?"

"Please."

While Shiloh propped himself against the table and held his hand up at her eye level, she quietly opened the door and peered out to see if there were any more patients waiting. The place was deserted. She turned back to find him staring at her.

"This ain't much of an office for you."

"Well," she said as she bent over his hand once more, "it's the best I've got. The locals don't seem overly keen on offering anything more, and I can't afford anything more at the moment. It's possible no one but the saloon keepers want me, and all they want is a steady supply of silver for the doves."

"Silver? For the diseases?"

"Colloidal silver, yes, for their diseases."

"They've got a tough life, I reckon." He hesitated. "I don't go in there, if that's what you're thinking."

She peered up at him, her hand in midair with the tweezers. "You just did, didn't you? I saw you in an argument with that man before I left. Or did you just happen to fall through a window?"

"I mean…" He cleared his throat. "I don't go in there for anything more than a drink."

"I see. Well, Mr. Coltrane, to be perfectly frank it's none of my business, nor do I care, what your personal preferences are in that regard."

"So you don't care about your patients?"

She picked out a small piece of glass, leaving a dot of blood, which she then swabbed with the carbolic.

Shiloh gritted his teeth and let out an "Owwwww!"

"I do care for my patients, but your personal life is none of my business unless you care to share it with me for some reason, a medical reason preferably."

"I did just share my personal life with you. And I'd think it was fairly medical."

She straightened once more, her gaze meeting his. "Left hand, please. Then you can take down your pants."

His thin lips curved slowly into a smile.

"My pleasure." He extended his left hand as if he were offering something, and she supported it underneath.

Something charged and exciting shot through her at touching him, as if it might burn her. She felt herself shake.

The size of his hands struck her. He must be well over six foot. Such well-formed hands, long fingers. There was some dirt under the nails, but the hands were reasonably clean, no doubt protected by his gloves when he rode. Calloused, rough, as if he worked hard.

"You don't make much conversation," he suddenly spat out.

She glanced up at him before extracting another piece of glass and dropping it with a faint clink in the basin, now placed beside him on the table.

She ignored his question but asked, "Your leg's hurting you. That position can't be comfortable."

"I'm fine. And I'll be lying down shortly, won't I?"

"You will be. Now. Let me see if I can figure what's stuck in your…backside."

Shiloh turned and leaned forward, supporting himself with both hands on the table.

She squatted a bit to try to see what might be prickling him, resisting the urge to run her hands over the fabric covering his buttocks. She stood.

"All right. I don't see anything. It's possible something stuck you and you feel that cut now, like a paper cut, if you've ever had one. I suggest you slowly—very slowly—push down your pants, and we'll see what happens."

He seemed to snort.

"You are wearing some sort of undergarment, aren't you?"

"A union suit."

"Great. Up on the table and—"

"I got the idea."

She picked up the basin and placed it on the chair, turning away to give him privacy. She listened as his boots dropped to the floor, followed by the sound of the heavy material of the jeans coming down and the groan of the table as it took his weight.

"Ready," he said.

She turned and bit her lip so hard she thought it might have drawn blood. Red. His union suit was red, and he was lying with his head resting on his crossed arms. She had to bite the inside of her cheek to stop from giggling, something not in her nature to do. For a moment, she wondered if she'd be able to proceed, then straightened her back and stood by the table, peering down at her patient's buttocks, still covered in the union suit. This was not what she had bargained for when she went through the medical college in Philadelphia—a barroom brawl and some cowboy's backside.

"I don't see anything. Can you point to where you think the glass might be?"

Shiloh propped himself up on one elbow and reached around, not without some awkwardness, and touched a spot on his behind.

Sydney delicately pulled up the fabric with both hands, stretching it away from his skin. "Is that any better?"

"Nope."

She sighed. "Then it must be in your skin; it's not

in the fabric."

"Great."

"I'm going to…have to…unbutton the access hatch."

The cowboy cupped his head in his hand and stared at her.

Was that a smile?

"Be my guest."

She unbuttoned the hatch as if it were burning her fingers and folded the flap so as not to be looking at any more than she need be. With evident relief in her voice, she said, "I see it." It was difficult not to think, as she took the tweezers and tried to grip the splinter of glass, he had a rear made completely of iron muscle. She couldn't stop the thought that if she touched that cheek, it would be hard as rock. These were thoughts she didn't want but couldn't help. Finally, the offending glass rang in the tin basin and she stepped back. "I better have a look at your face when you get your pants back on. Let me just swab this so it doesn't get infected."

"Are you sure there's no more?" There was a slight hint of sarcasm mixed with a vague amusement in his tone.

"You tell me. Do you feel anything else?"

"Guess I'll see when I sit again, but for now I don't feel a thing."

As she turned to get the carbolic she could feel his gaze on her. There was a sort of contained anger about the man, a danger, and a wariness that resonated with her. She turned back to find him studying her once more.

"What made you become a doctor? Not a

particularly usual profession for a woman."

"I was always interested in…"

"Bodies?"

She swabbed the spot where she had extracted the glass. "You can get dressed now, and I'll look at your face." She pivoted away. "And no, it wasn't an interest in bodies. Why is it, do you think, it's all right for a man to look at a woman's body, deliver babies and so on, but not all right for a woman to look at a man's?"

"You seem rather embarrassed by it, for a start."

She swirled around to face him just as he buttoned his jeans. Her reaction brought another thin smile to his face.

"See what I mean?"

"No, I do not see what you mean. I am not embarrassed."

"Mine the first man's body you've dealt with? Other than a cadaver, of course."

She straightened her shoulders. "I'm not going to answer that, Mr. Coltrane. If you're not pleased with my service you can, as I said earlier, go see the barber."

"I'm pleased. At least I can sit now. I think." He propped himself up on the table once more and faced her. He nodded confirmation his rear was fine. "Difficult to stand in the saddle all the way home."

Exasperated, she grabbed up her tweezers once more, and the basin. "Let me look at your face."

She could see the thin smile he tried to stop as she took hold of his chin and turned his head to the left. There was the white line of a graze she hadn't noticed before; it ran diagonally from his sideburn, and his shaggy hair must've hidden it. "A bullet graze?"

"Yup."

"Quarter of an inch to the left and you'd have lost your eye."

"But I didn't."

She picked out three small shards, stood back, and turned his face to the center once more. "There's one right above your lip I'm going to have to get out."

"With your…" Seeing her color rise, he seemed to think better of whatever he was going to say. "Thank you."

She leant in to better see the glass. It looked like a bead of sweat on his lip, and she could see the individual hairs of the coming beard, fair against his skin, feel his breath on her face. She wondered if this was what a kiss was like, then banished the thought and concentrated on her work. But his gaze was boring into her, and she pondered if he thought something similar, that it was as if they were going to kiss. Her hand shook and she stood back.

"You're doing fine. Go on, I won't bite you."

She looked away and then back to work, pulled the splinter out, and cupped his chin once more, working on his left side now as his face turned to the right.

"It's getting dark. How far do you have to get home?"

"I'll be fine, Mr. Coltrane. I'm used to riding in the dark."

"That may be, but it doesn't make it sensible or right."

"I assure you I can take care of myself." She turned away to put her items back in her bag.

Coltrane stood and grabbed her arm, just hard enough that she knew she couldn't get away.

"Ow! You're hurting me! How dare you!"

"Lady, I'm just proving a point here. If I could get hold of you, so could any man."

"Don't be ridiculous! You're standing right behind me. I'm going to be on a fast horse with a gun."

"The horse has a gun?"

She yanked her arm away. "Very funny. Now if you don't mind, I think we're finished here, and you can head home and I'll head back."

Her patient hung his head for a moment. "Bozy says you work at the reservation."

"What about it?"

"With the soldiers around and all?"

"Mr. Coltrane! Please don't concern yourself about my welfare; where I live and where I work is none of your affair!"

"Maybe not, but I—"

Her fury at him and what he had done to her, not only grabbing her but making her think things, have feelings she didn't want, made her shake. "I'd like you to go now, please. We're through here."

Coltrane's chest expanded with the depth of his breath. "Fine. Guess I must owe you something for your work. How much?"

She pivoted away from him. "It's fine. No one pays."

"That doesn't make it right. Surely you must get something."

"What folks can. Produce or baking, help on my cabin, whatever. So just leave what you can, if it makes you happy, and go."

"Nothing much makes me happy, but what's right is right. What do you think your time is worth?"

"What do I think my time is worth? Do I include

the years I spent studying so I know how to treat people, the time wasted with a bunch of cowboys coming in to gawp at me, the hours standing up to insults? What do *you* think that is worth?"

He stood there for what seemed like minutes, studying her face, as if he were waiting to see if she would cry. In a voice so soft she could barely hear him, he said, "Well, I guess I haven't got enough money to cover all that." He reached into his back pocket and slipped out some change, grabbed his hat up and slapped it on his head. "There you go." He took her hand, palm up, and laid two coins in it as he swung toward the door.

She stared down at the half-eagles in her hand. "That's far too much."

Coltrane opened the door and faced her.

"Not to me it isn't. Worth every penny."

Chapter Two

Damn woman.

She was taking a road through a wooded area and Shiloh knew if he didn't stay back enough she'd hear him. Heck, it was nigh on impossible not to be heard, with the fallen trees and branches the horse was dealing with, the early leaf fall like sponge underfoot, twigs crackling, and stones being thrown by moving hooves.

Fast-moving clouds hid the crescent moon.

He wondered why he was doing this. What was she to him anyway? He had promised himself he wouldn't get involved with a woman, or anyone for that matter, until he had strung up his no-good brother-in-law and found the men who had murdered his sister and her child. He couldn't see himself leading any kind of life until those men had paid with theirs.

Anger coursed through him. His ranch was off to the east now, and the doctor was headed west. His road home would be a long one. Getting into the fight with Ike had been dumb, but sometimes the anger just came over him in a wave, a hot seething fury so he'd do anything to rile just about anyone, and Ike had been his target this time.

A branch cracked somewhere off to the side, and he pulled his Colt.

"You're not a very good tracker, are you?" Her voice came through the darkness as if it were part of the night air, blanketing him lightly so he felt calmer in that moment, more at ease.

He holstered his gun.

"I know you're following me and I don't know why you're doing this, but I wish you'd go. Go back to your own place. Leave me alone."

He tried to make out her features, but she was back behind a tree, obviously not afraid of him, which surprised him. Her horse grazed for a moment on some scrub as if he had decided to have a late night treat, not mindful of what the humans were up to.

"Well? You seemed to have enough to say back in my office."

"How did you know?"

"Like I said: you're not a very good tracker. I could hear someone behind me."

"How did you know it was me, then? I might have been someone out to get you, a bandit—or worse."

"And I told you I was fine on my own. You don't seem able to listen. Maybe I should have checked your hearing."

"I don't like the thought of a woman—any woman—riding out on her own at night. It's not safe, it's—"

"Isn't that for the woman—me—to decide? It's none of your business, Mr. Coltrane. And you've just had a pile of glass removed from your skin. My advice to you is to head on home and get some rest. Get some sleep. And forget about me."

"I can't." He realized those words had two meanings in his mind, one of them nothing to do with her getting home safely.

"You can't? Seems simple enough."

"Maybe. But I wouldn't rest easy thinking you might be in trouble."

The doctor pulled her horse's head up sharply and moved in closer to him. Sudden moonlight flickered through the branches overhead, and he could see her face now, stern, a wary set to her jaw and eyes.

"I'm gonna see you to your door and then leave. Promise."

"Do you know how stupid this is? Are you going to see me home tomorrow night, and the night after, and the night after that?"

"You in town all those nights? I thought you came down once a week."

She sighed with a deep frustration. "All right. Is this going to be your once-a-week ritual then? Because if it is, I'm just going to close up shop and let folks come out here if they want to see me. Makes more sense anyway, the way things are going."

"I can't help get you more patients, I'm afraid, but I can try to see you're safe." His brows arched, daring her to reject him.

"So you're a self-appointed bodyguard or something."

She took a breath, and he sensed her study the hard planes of his face, the steel in his eyes.

"Why me? Why don't you find some other woman on her own to look after?"

"I don't know any other woman who needs looking after. *You* do."

"How arrogant! You've decided I need saving from some unknown killer or outlaw or something, and so you've taken it upon yourself to save me from him. Have I got that right?"

"As I said, I don't know anyone else who needs saving, but it seems to me you might. You're taking chances riding up here on your own, doing what you do."

She leaned in to him so he could feel the warmth coming off her body, saw now she was wearing a slouch hat and her hair was up.

"Why are you dressed like a man if you think you're so safe?"

She sat back, her shoulders slumping.

He sensed her resignation, watched as she pulled her horse around the tree behind which she had hidden, and got back on the trail. He pulled up beside her as she went on. And stayed there.

****

"Home. I'd like to see you ride off now, please."

"I'll ride off, but I want to ask you: what difference would it make if I said no? Or if I rode off and circled back? You think you're safe here? On your own? I showed you in the office what could happen. So what do you think your pleasant little request would do if I, or anyone else, didn't feel like riding off? What would you do then?"

She pulled the knife so fast she knew he'd hardly seen her hand move. It had taken a lot of practice to learn to do, but practice she had. And she knew just how to use it.

"An Arkansas toothpick? Is that what that is?"

"If that's what you call it. Back east we just called it a clasp-knife. You see, this one springs out. And before you ask, yes, I know how to use it. I studied surgery, after all."

"I bet you did, but…"

She closed the knife and slid down from her horse. "I'm tired of this conversation, Mr. Coltrane. I'd appreciate it if you headed off now." She started to undo the cinch on her horse and pulled the saddle, swinging it over the rail of her fence.

"Tell me one thing—"

She swiveled back to him, squinting across at him on his horse, the moon just lighting his features so she could see his darkening beard and some of the scrapes and nicks from the glass. "No, you tell me one thing!"

"All right. What?"

She knew from his snarl he wasn't going to be happy about answering, whatever her question was.

"Why?"

"Why what?"

"Why, really, are you following me?"

Coltrane made the slightest movement in his saddle as if he were getting more comfortable. His breathing got more pronounced but his hands were still on the reins as he glowered down at her. She could hear him make a decisive smack with his mouth, but still he didn't reply. He looked away as if he were considering what to do, then pivoted back to her.

"My sister inherited our ranch from my father. My father thought I was a good-for-nothing—"

"And are you?"

"Probably. Maybe then. Maybe not so much now."

"So?"

"She then married a man, Oswald Parmeter was his name, maybe *is* his name if the bastard's still alive. Had a child by him. A *real* good-for-nothing who fell in with a bunch of other no-goods, outlaws. Parmeter left her on the ranch. Alone. With the child. Then one night—"

"I don't think I want to hear the rest."

"No, 'course you don't. You know what happened, and you know it could happen to you."

She moved around her horse to stand just below him and peered up at him. "Mr. Coltrane, I'm not your sister, the outlaws aren't coming back here. You have to get on home now."

He ignored her. "They killed both her and the child, those animals. For what? For what reason? As far as anyone can make out, it was because Parmeter had run off with some of their money or something and it was their revenge. He told them, I believe, if he inherited the ranch and some money she had, he could pay them back."

She felt sick. Men who could kill a child and a woman really were animals. Just as he said. She clasped her forehead, then glanced back up at him. "Where...where were you when this happened?"

He snorted. "I was just as my father said I was: good for nothing. I came back to make a fresh start shortly after and heard the whole thing. The town doesn't like me much because I asked too many questions, stirred up their shame. Not to mention I went round every damn ranch in the area and got our herd back. Most of them had used a running iron to change the brand, but it was plain as day. Others had felt sorry the cattle weren't being seen to, were honest people, and handed them over. So now I'm waiting."

"Waiting?"

"Waiting to decide what to do next. Waiting to see if those bastards come on back. Or Parmeter comes back to claim what I guess is rightly his—my ranch. As her legal husband it should be his, but I'll be damned and in my grave before I let him have it."

Sydney got hold of her horse's bridle and swung the reins over his head to lead him to his stall. She turned back to Coltrane as she opened her gate. "Get home, Mr. Coltrane, and stop worrying—or even thinking—about me. I've managed to get myself here and can look out for myself. Seems like you've got other things to worry about. I'm fine."

She could just hear him mumble, "Last words," as he reined his horse to the east and headed home.

Sydney realized she had never thought of outlaws or bandits or whatever the heck they called them out here. She had just wanted to get away from the east and her humiliations in wanting to be a doctor, the way her parents had more or less disinherited her, and being forced to take advantage of the kindness of her professor and his wife, another female doctor. She'd known she could never repay them, but she could make them proud and feel they had accomplished what they had set out to do—make her an outstanding practitioner, serving patients who needed her. Iona, the wife, had passed on now, and relations with Garnforth, the professor, had become complicated, but her feeling of indebtedness hadn't gone.

The cabin was something the Agency let her have, near enough to the reservation but far away enough for her not to be a temptation to the soldiers at the fort. Somewhere in her was a belief soldiers were upstanding, kept the peace, served the good, and would hardly do anything so crass and wrong as to take advantage of a woman. Surely, they knew their commanding officer would deal sharply with them if they even tried. But their words, their language, even the ignorance of the wives who were there and shunned her—that was most puzzling. The women preferred having a male doctor look to their needs rather than a "disgraceful" woman.

The door creaked open and she dropped her bag to get hold of the lantern, opened the glass, and struck one of her Diamond matches by feel until the flame blossomed and she lit the wick. The sound of the glass hitting the rim as she replaced it relieved the quiet for a moment before she plopped her hat on the table and turned to the basin whose water had chilled during the day. Too tired to go out and get fresh and heat it, she grabbed the soap and scrub brush and scrubbed her hands before washing her face. As she leant over the basin, she recalled Shiloh Coltrane, the feel of his breath on her face, the hands that seemed almost elegant—too elegant for a man like that—and his resolve she be safe. She found it difficult to think straight, to sort her feelings about a man who insisted on seeing her home safely while he projected the hard countenance and isolation of a loner. It was a conundrum.

She undressed and changed for bed, slipped between the covers, but it was Shiloh Coltrane's face she saw in front of her, Shiloh Coltrane's voice she heard. And Shiloh Coltrane's warning that echoed in her mind.

****

Shiloh drifted off to sleep every few paces home until his horse would stumble and he'd shake himself awake, pull up the horse's head, and give the gelding his spur once more. He wanted his own bed, and he figured Bones would stay up until he got in, and Bones would've seen to his stock and had the cabin warm, and maybe a meal waiting. He knew he took advantage of the man, though he tried his best to do his share. And now he had another worry: he just could not get that woman out of his mind. Even asleep he seemed to be thinking of her, seeing her face, hearing her voice. He didn't need any complications, he kept telling himself—the ranch was enough with his intentions to find those men. He had it up and running and Bones looking after things; time to go after them when he found who and where they were.

But how? That was it. He had hoped Parmeter would show up one day and lead him to them, but Parmeter hadn't come. Not yet. And Shiloh felt he was wasting his time.

A light glowed in the window, and for a moment, he sat the horse whose restlessness reminded him he wouldn't get into the warmth of his cabin until he'd seen to Whiskey. The animal nickered his impatience, and Shiloh could make out Bones peering through the window. He slithered down from his saddle and stood for a moment.

"Well, what the heck happened to you, Boss? I was 'spectin' you hours ago." Bones pulled the door shut behind him as he faced his employer.

He turned so Bones could see his face. Then he pulled Whiskey's cinch loose and grabbed his saddle.

"Who done that?" Bones asked, hands on hips.

"A window."

"I see. And I suppose it just fell out of its frame on its own and come right up to ya, cut ya up, and held ya down for sev'ral hours."

Shiloh gave a glance to his ranch hand, the moon giving the dark brown of his skin a sheen like polished wood, the whites of his eyes bright in the darkness. The old man stood waiting for a reply.

"Got the doc to fix me up."

"Since when we have a doctor in town?" When there was no reply, he continued, "Doc must've taken his sweet time. It's long past supper now, you know that?"

He almost flung his saddle and blanket at Bones and led his horse into the barn, the ranch hand on his heels. He took the bridle off and got the feed while Bones set the saddle on its rack, pulled the blanket free, and gave it a shake before throwing it over its holder. Shiloh started to curry Whiskey.

"I guess there's somethin' I'm not bein' told here."

"I guess there is."

"Your silence speaks volumes, Boss, you know that?"

"So what is it saying to you?"

"It's saying you done somethin' real dumb, that's what."

Shiloh let himself guffaw, turned his head to gaze at Bones for a moment before pivoting back to the horse's flank.

"Yah. It's a woman."

"I thought as much. One of them doves finally get to you?"

"The doc. The doc is a woman."

Bones shook his head. "That don't make no sense. How can a doctor be a woman?"

As Shiloh moved around the horse he thought about that but didn't reply for a moment. "Just is," he said at last. "Guess she studied and all and became a doctor."

"Humph." Bones reached behind Shiloh as he came out of the stall and closed the door. "That there's jus' the kind of woman you don't need to get involved with."

"I don't intend to."

Chapter Three

"They're starving!" Sydney's hands balled into fists at her sides but she felt like using them to take a swing at this obstinate, uncaring, *deaf* Indian Agent, Manfred Morris. "They were supposed to get a shipment of food! Where is it?"

Morris looked up at her, disapproval if not revulsion written on his face. "The shipment is late," he said succinctly.

"And so you intend just to let them starve to death."

"Miss Cantrell—" he started between gritted teeth.

"It's '*Doctor*' if you don't mind! I did the same course as a man and I am entitled to the same respect."

Morris raised his gaze to her and stared for a moment before continuing. "*Doctor* Cantrell. The situation is beyond my control. The Army accompanies the shipment up from Cheyenne. As far as I know, according to a wire I received, the shipment arrived. The Army has not as yet reached us. There is nothing I can do." He seemed to have an aura of weariness about him, as if the subject had been gone over numerous times.

"Nothing you can do! I find that difficult to believe, Mr. Morris, when you are sitting here well-fed and the people you look after out there are starving."

"Miss...Doctor Cantrell, I am one person. I cannot

go riding off and bring an entire unit of cavalry back to the reservation. They—"

"They're probably eating the food themselves, or unloading it at the fort."

"I sincerely doubt that. They get their own provisions."

"They do it just to starve these people. You know they do!"

"I know no such thing. If I did, I would certainly talk with their commanding officer."

"Then why don't you?"

"You may be aware that an Indian Agent is no longer under the jurisdiction of the Army. We are no longer under the Department of War; we are under the Department of the Interior. The Army was not favorable to this change and resents us. They resent us, I might say, about as much as you do. Therefore, if I use my position unnecessarily it will only bring more resentment. I save these conflicts for when absolutely necessary." He reached for a glass of water and drank, then shuffled around some papers on his desk.

The room was smoky, the windows dirty, the air fetid. She thought she might retch if she didn't get out. "And you don't think starvation makes it necessary?"

"I'm sorry, Doctor, there is nothing I can do. I suggest you see to your patients and do the best you can for them. As soon as provisions arrive, I shall distribute them and all will be well."

She gasped at the blatant lie, the nonsense of it, but knew there was no point in continuing here. She was wasting her time while patients were lining up outside the shack she had as an office. She gave Morris a hard stare before swiveling on her heel and yanking the door open.

Outside she bent over to catch her breath, contain herself, and breathe in the fresh air. The taut faces of those anticipating her care stared with listless expressions, unblinking eyes, emaciated hands pulling their blankets tight about them against a stiff wind. And she knew now, from having treated them for several weeks, all they would want were the tonics the mule train brought in, tonics with the merest hint of alcohol and laudanum that relaxed them and for some short time made them forget their loss, the inhumanity that had been cast upon them.

She walked to her office like the condemned to the gallows.

****

Shiloh didn't think much of barbed wire, but it was inescapable now, ubiquitous across the prairie. He recalled days in his youth when he could ride for hours without a fence across open range, the prairie unmarked by the divisions of ranches, private property, trespass laws, with cattle grazing, and wild animals, mustangs coming through. But he also remembered the winter of 1886-7 and his father riding out with the hands, searching for stock they might be able to save, coming back half-frozen, broken men, most of the cattle gone or dead. That was more than ten years ago, and his father hadn't let him and his sister help despite being in their teen years; they'd waited by a fire with their mother, trusting their father would somehow return with good news.

He snapped the wire that had come down and got a length from his roll, walked the rod distance, and started to fix it back up. Across the pasture, Bones was herding some strays into the main group and then something else caught his eye on the far horizon. A horseman riding fast his way.

Only it wasn't a horseman. It was a horsewoman.

"Ow. Damn!" The surprise left him not knowing what he was doing and he caught a barb on his forearm, a cut now running up his sleeve and arm. "Damn!"

He pressed the open skin to stop the bleeding but couldn't pull his eyes away from the rider, long hair flying out behind her, her hat on its stampede string bouncing behind, the chestnut horse at a gallop coming his way. He gave a glance toward Bones to see if he had noticed. Yup, nothing escaped that old man; he sat his mount like a bronze statue watching the doctor ride in.

"How'd you find me?" he asked before she had barely stopped.

She caught her breath before sliding down from the horse and approached him, noted his hand stanching the cut on his arm. "Looks like I got here just in time." Her voice was mild, somewhat amused, as she switched back to her bag tied on the rear of her saddle. "Bozy in the saloon told me where you lived."

"And to what do I owe the honor? You're surely not checking my cuts from the other day."

The doctor scrambled in her bag and brought up a bottle and some bandaging.

"I don't need that. It's not a deep cut."

"No, you, of course, would prefer to get septicemia."

"What's that?"

"An infection from which you can die. Blood poisoning."

31

"I'm not ready to die and—"

She grabbed his arm to look at it. "Lucky for you, it looks fairly superficial. How're your cuts from the glass?"

"Is that why you came? To check how I'm doing?"

She shook the bottle, meeting his gaze, then opened it, put some of the liquid on the bandage. "Can you push your shirt sleeve back, please?"

He did what he was asked and snorted slightly at the bossiness of the woman. "Happy?"

"Very." She began to wipe the cut.

"So what's that, then?"

"Solution of carbolic. It works to disinfect and prevent infection."

He watched her concentration on what she was doing, peered at her with a small smile he couldn't stop. "You haven't answered my question."

She looked up, then completed her task, silently bandaging the cut. "No, I didn't actually come to see how you were doing, though I suppose I should have. Any of those cuts giving you pain, feel raw, are swollen?"

"Nope. A bit of itchiness is all."

"Good. Keep them and this new one clean." She wiped the bottle with a cloth from her pocket and got the cap back on, pivoted back to the bag on her horse, her back to him. "Actually, I came to ask you a favor."

"A favor."

"Yes." She swiveled back to him, her hands loose at her sides. "I need a cow."

For a moment, he didn't say anything, pressed down the desire to laugh at her, got hold of himself. "A cow."

"Do you always repeat everything someone says?"

"I don't think so, but you come up with some statements, or ideas, I find perplexing. What in tarnation do you want a cow for? Or do you mean a steer?"

"What's the difference?"

He guffawed and shook his head. "How long you lived out here again?"

Her hands found her hips, and she kicked one leg of her divided skirt away. "Not long."

"Humph." He spied Bones riding over to them, no doubt curious as to what was going on.

Bones' gaze shifted from one to the other before he leant down, his hand out toward the doctor. "Howdy. Name's Bones."

The doctor readily shook the proffered hand. "Sydney Cantrell."

"Miss...Doctor Cantrell saw to my cuts the other day."

"Uh-hmm." Bones sat back in his saddle and studied the woman before he gave Shiloh a sideways glance. "I see. Well, now. I better be gettin' on back to those strays." His eyes slid once more to Shiloh with arched brows and a smirk on his face. "Nice to meet you, ma'am. Doctor. I hope we'll cross paths again. Maybe when Mr. Coltrane is feelin' a bit more hospitable."

They stood in silence and watched him ride off.

Shiloh bit his lip. "I think he was telling me I should be asking you in for coffee or maybe *tea* or something. Homestead's just over there."

"That's not necessary, and I really can't stay anyway."

"No, you want to get back to that dangerous cabin of yours."

She sighed. "It really isn't your concern."

"You've said that before. I get it. So now, this cow? You want a milk cow?"

"No, I want a beef cow for the Indians. They're starving. The soldiers who were supposed to escort their provisions up from Cheyenne have not arrived and there's hardly any food available to them. I thought if I could get beef…" Her forehead wrinkled, no doubt thinking how ridiculous she was being.

"And you gonna slaughter this beef yourself? Take the hide, dress the animal, cut it up into portions, maybe even cook it?" He crossed his arms, his mouth puckered. "Or you expecting this cow comes ready and I just got it stored away, ready to hand out for charity?"

She spun back to her mount. "All right. I see there was no point in coming here. I thought…I thought with all your concern about my well-being it might extend to other people, people who really need help." She took hold of her saddle horn and put her foot in the stirrup.

"Hang on. I didn't say I wouldn't help. I'm just pointing out to you the problems involved. And, by the way, they're steers if it's beef you're wanting. Not cows."

She twisted back to him, her foot back down on soil as she studied her boots. "So what's the difference?"

He shook his head. "Steers are the grown calves we've…we've…castrated." He bit his lip again. *Could you say that to a lady, even if she was a doctor?* "They fatten up. Cows are the females." He pulled down the sleeve where she had bandaged his arm. "And they

34

don't come ready to eat."

The doctor stood up straight. "I think the women know all about dressing an animal, treating the hide and so on. Haven't they been doing it for thousands of years?"

"Probably. But not beef, not that it matters. I guess if they can dress buffalo and deer and elk and so on, they can dress a steer."

"So can I buy one?"

Her glare bore into him but he met her gaze.

"How much? What do you get for a steer, if you don't mind my asking?"

"Depends. Depends on the market. At the moment, not much. Fifteen year ago I might've said sixty dollars. Now it's more like twenty-three." He didn't tell her the price per pound once delivered to Chicago. It wasn't worth it. "Cattle's a dying business." He studied her. They said there were now over sixty thousand people in Wyoming. Sixty thousand! And with all those, he had to meet *her*. "What've you got?"

She scrabbled in her pocket and pulled out the two half-eagles he'd given her, flat palm displaying the pieces.

He almost laughed.

"But that's a down payment. I can owe you the rest."

He turned back to his fence and started to fix it again.

"Please. I *will* pay you back. I promise."

"Yeah, I'm sure you will, Doctor. But how you gonna get that single steer up to the reservation? How you gonna herd it all that way on your own?"

"I...I thought maybe—"

"You thought I'd just run on up there and deliver it for you?"

"No! I thought I could just herd it. You could tell me how. Don't you just sort of push it along with your horse? I saw Bones over there getting some cattle to join the herd."

"Bones has some forty years' experience. A single steer'll just run off. You'd never get him where you want, running over the range." He dropped his tools and twisted back to her once more. "You said you wanted a favor."

"Yes. I meant for you to sell me the cow and let me repay you when I can."

"Why're you doing this? What are those people to you anyway? Other than your patients, I guess."

Her color rose and he could see her fight to get hold of her anger.

"They're *humans*, Mr. Coltrane. They're humans and they're starving. That's what they are to me."

"And what're you eating if there's no food?"

"I get provisions in town. And I told you: my patients pay me in produce and so on, and I grow a bit as well." She took up the reins of her horse and swung into the saddle. "Anyway, it was just an idea." Her voice was more subdued now. "Thanks for the lesson on cows versus steers." She pulled her horse's head around and galloped off.

"I didn't say…" But it was no use. She was gone and didn't hear him. "I didn't say you couldn't do it," he mumbled to himself, and took up his wire clipper once more.

****

Bones got it out of him, one word at a time.

"She wants to feed the Injuns?"

"Yup."

"And wanted you to give her a steer, let her herd it on over to the reservation?"

"Yup."

"So whatcha gonna do? You cain't jus' let her do it alone."

"I didn't say I was going to do anything, or let her have one."

"So you's goin' to let them peoples die? They starvin' an' all."

Shiloh took a deep breath and poured them each a mug of coffee. He slammed Bones' mug down in front of him; a spot of coffee landed on the table. The old man squinted up, one leg crossed over the other, his fingers tapping out his impatience. Shiloh glanced around his homestead, a tidy, comfortable place his sister had made into a fine home before she was murdered. Almost too comfortable with rag rugs on the floor she had woven and pillows she had sewn, daily reminders Shiloh wasn't avenging her death, wasn't making much of an effort to find her murderer.

The truth was, he just didn't know where to start. He had asked around and reached a dead end. And people probably felt threatened by him, by his reputation, didn't want much to do with him still.

He looked into the black pool of coffee as if he were reading his fortune, but only the reflection of the light found its way through the window, came back at him. He glanced up at Bones. "So you think I should take her the damn steer?"

"You know, there's something I've realized 'bout you, Coltrane."

"Oh, yeah, what's that?"

"Aside from your past, or maybe despite it, you have a good heart. You took me on when few would, you's concerned 'bout people, and far as I know, you never done kilt no one what didn't need killing."

"Humph. So what's your point?"

Bones swigged back his coffee and rose with the sluggishness of his age, of his long day, of his work. "Well. I'll bet you anything you won't sleep tonight."

He was right.

Shiloh tossed and turned through the night, the image of the woman haunting him, voices in his head demanding what he would do, both to help the doctor and retaliate for the death of his sister and her child.

In the morning he cut three steers out of his herd. Bones sat his horse and watched, shook his head. Shiloh heard the old man laugh as he rode off.

****

As he entered the encampment, his gaze caught sight of her. Giggling. Now that was a turn-up. He hadn't thought her capable of laughter, always so serious with him. Stern. Her laughter rang like chimes in the wind as she lifted a young child and swung him in the air. Two Indian women watched, smiles just crinkling their eyes.

She said something to them he couldn't hear. She was still unaware of him, but as the cattle lowed, she turned her head in surprise, gaped up at him, her mouth slightly open as she held the child. And for one brief moment he wanted some things he had never even let himself think of—a wife, a child, his home, peace.

He sat waiting.

The doctor set the little boy back on the ground,

gave his head an absentminded pat as she continued to take in Shiloh and his three steers. With almost hesitant steps she came over to him, gazed up. She put her hand on his leg, then pulled it back as if she'd suddenly realized it was too personal a gesture.

"I…I don't know what to say." Her gaze searched his face.

" 'Thank you' will do." He got down from his horse, the reins in his hand. He could feel her breath, and he so wanted to kiss her in that moment. The gratitude on her face held him there.

She shook her head in agreement. "Thank you. I don't know how to pay you, but thank you. I'll repay you somehow." She blinked, maybe disconcerted by the fact he couldn't stop staring at her. "How much do I actually owe you?"

"You don't. It's payment for your tending my cut yesterday and on account with you for any future attention I may need." *Future attention? Well.* "Where do you want them?"

She glanced around and spotted the corral. "I guess in there?"

"There are horses in there. Are you sure? They don't always get on at first."

The muscle of her jaw clenched as she considered, then she ran over to an elderly man who'd just come out of one of the cabins. She gestured excitedly and the man nodded several times. Something in Shiloh's heart exploded, and he ached, literally ached, felt bruised, and his face crumbled.

She ran back to him.

"What's wrong?" Her tone was excited, happy. "You can't know how happy this has made them.

They're going to deal with it, watch them. Thank you. Thank you so much."

He could barely shake his head in response. Finally, he got out, "So you want them in the corral, I take it."

"Yes, please."

A low light surrounded them, late afternoon, hints of stars in a pale blue sky. The moon hung like some Christmas ornament, and the evening air chilled slightly. She pulled her wrap about her as he re-mounted and headed the grazing steers through the corral gate, which the elderly man swung open for him. He nodded down at the Indian as he passed.

"Gep, gep, gep. Gep, gep, gep." As one tried to get away, he maneuvered his horse quickly to get the steer into the pen. When all three were in, the Indian swung the gate closed, nodded his thanks with a slight smile to Shiloh.

She came up beside him. In the dimming light, he could barely make out her features but was sure her eyes sparkled.

"You headed home?" he asked.

"Yes."

"Then I better ride with you."

She had no idea what to make of this man, but blood pounded in her veins when she was near him. She recalled the taut arms, the lines of sinew as he'd stretched out and pushed his shirtsleeve up for her to treat him, the fine blond hairs. And those hands, the long elegant fingers. She thought of the lines around his mouth and eyes, slightly aging him perhaps beyond his years, and that scar that ran from his sideburn covered by the unkempt hair. There was some loneliness in him that spoke to her, marked by an inner sadness, yet at the same time, he seemed loath to show his compassion.

They rode in a companionable silence, lost in their thoughts.

"Bones. How did you meet Bones? I take it he works for you. Did he just show up one day?"

"Nope."

She waited, wondered if he thought she was nosy, or chatty, or peculiar somehow, suddenly bringing up his hired hand.

Coltrane took a deep breath. "Met him down in Texas a few years back."

She glanced across at him as they rode. Was this all he was going to say?

"I see."

"They were beating him. For no reason. Just plain orneriness because he's black."

"Oh. That's awful."

"Yup."

She pondered this. "You stopped them, I take it."

"Why do you say that?" He squinted across at her, suspicion written on his face, flint in his eyes.

"Because I doubt any decent person would just stand there, watch, and not do anything."

"Yeah. I stopped it. Then we rode together for a bit, 'til I decided to come on back home. Bones came with me."

"I see."

He reined in his horse and gazed across at her as she stopped beside him. "Thing is, I don't think you do see. I don't think... Never mind." He kicked his horse to trot on.

She caught up. "Well, I can't see, I can't

understand if you don't tell me." Frustrated with him, she reached across to pull on his rein.

His anger flashed like a burst of lightning. "You do that and a horse can rear. Then what would happen? Probably you, not me, would get thrown because I'm prepared for it but you, you're not, you're leaning out of your saddle and your horse is going to spook. You ever think of that?"

"Sorry. I just—"

"I shot them. That's what I did. I shot the bastards. Two of them. Now you see?"

She reined her horse again. "But...you probably saved his life. And it was wrong, what they were doing, I mean. You don't go around just shooting people. In this instance, they probably deserved it. It was probably the only thing you could do if Bones was incapacitated. It would be two against one." She knew she sounded as if she were pleading, wanting that to have been the case, that there had been no other possibility except for him to kill the two men.

Coltrane shook his head. "I could've shot them in the leg or the shoulder to get them to stop. And they're not the first, you should know that. They're not the first, nor likely to be the last. When I find my sister's murderers, I'll be killing them, too."

"I..." She started to say they probably deserved it but knew that wasn't what she felt. He shouldn't be judge, jury, and executioner all in one. He should bring them to justice. "Couldn't you just...just bring them to the sheriff?"

"What? And let them break out of jail, or worm their way out of prison, not enough evidence or something, or maybe they get themselves some fancy lawyer."

"Well, that's not likely now, is it?"

"I don't know. I don't know where they are. I don't know much about them, in fact. But when I find them, and I know for sure..." He glanced across at her once more. "This is where I head off. You want me to see you home? I think I should. It doesn't sit well with me to just leave you here in the dark."

"I'll make you some dinner. It's the least I can do."

Chapter Four

He checked the house, then said he'd see to the horses.

Sydney entered her cabin, thoughts stampeding through her mind, fighting with each other. She was a doctor, she healed people, did her best to save them if ill or hurt, helped them to live. Coltrane was a killer. He appeared to have little remorse—an angel of death was what she thought. No, from what she now understood, he didn't just go around shooting people. Or did he? Was he a hired gun? What did she know about this man?

His empathy for her, for the Indians—or *was* it empathy? Did he just do it to please her? Did he just feel bad because she had asked? What did she really know about Shiloh Coltrane?

"That was a big sigh," he said entering the cabin, entering her thoughts.

"I...I guess I'm a bit tired."

"Do you want me to go? Bones probably left me something anyway. If you're tired—"

"No. No, I'm happy for the company and, as I said, it's the least I can do. Give you a meal."

"You don't owe me anything. I said that." He leaned back against the door, crossed his arms.

"Yes, well, a meal is hardly payment, now is it?"

"And I said I don't need payment, I don't want

payment."

"There's a basin there. The water's fresh." She nodded toward her washbasin and pitcher.

He took the hint; his thin smile turned up his lips.

"I haven't got the best cut of beef, but I started this stew this morning, and I think it's good."

"I'm sure it is."

They both turned toward the window as two horsemen rode up.

She wiped her hands on her apron, met his questioning gaze. "Probably patients. I often get people come out here. Could you...go into the bedroom and stay there 'til I'm finished, or maybe go out through the back door there? I don't want anyone thinking... knowing I'm entertaining a man."

Her hands went to straighten her hair, and she untied her apron as her guest slipped into the back room. She peered out the window, couldn't see who it was, but felt safe with Coltrane there.

Two soldiers.

"Good evening. Are you lost?" She put iron in her voice. *They shouldn't be here; they have their own doctor.* The smell of alcohol wafted her way.

One seemed to almost be holding himself up on the frame of the door while the other leaned in, leered at her. "No, no."

Drunk as all-get-out. She took a step back.

"We need medical attention." They both laughed at this, a sly, insinuating guffaw. Their hot breaths came at her like a warning.

"You have your own medic at the fort. Can you go, please? Leave now. He'll see to you."

"Oh, we'll go." The leaning one shoved her aside

roughly and entered the cabin. "Smells good. You 'spectin' us for dinner?" His words slurred as he grinned; broken and black teeth added to his evil countenance.

She stood her ground, wondered if Coltrane was listening or had gone out the back to make sure he wasn't heard. They hadn't spotted the second horse, or maybe didn't know she didn't have two.

"I'm sure hungry, and this looks a helluva lot better than that slop they give us up at the fort." He grabbed a potholder and lifted the pot from the range. "Come on, Harley," he said to his cohort. "We have some dessert here." Again, there was the evil laugh.

"Dessert?" For a moment she didn't understand the implication, but as she swiveled to face him, the other drunk, Harley she presumed, came up behind her and grabbed her by both arms.

She struggled to get out of his stinking grasp. "Let me go! Let me go!"

"Oh, not before we have our main course. A little fun. Don't you want a little fun?"

He set the pot back on the range and came up to her, breathing heavily, as the other one held her.

"Lay her on the table, Harley. I want my—"

The back door slammed and all three pivoted toward the bedroom door.

Coltrane stood there, the barrel of his Colt pointed at the speaker's head.

"Let her go."

His low voice was so threatening, Sydney felt as if she were guilty of the intrusion.

"I said, let her go."

The two men froze in their tracks.

As Harley released her, he gave her a shove of disgust. "I told you she couldn't be single."

She moved away, straightened herself, but didn't meet Coltrane's gaze. Her breath came out in tremors. He'd be on to her about living out here, about living on her own; he'd feel he was proved correct, all his words about this solitary cabin and a woman on her own. And what if he hadn't been here tonight, now?

She finally found the wherewithal to glance at him. He bit his lip as if he were considering what to do. Then he gazed at her with raised brows. Questioning.

"Just get them out of here," she whispered. "They won't dare come back."

"Nope. And I'm thinking their commanding officer over at the fort will be interested to hear about this, as well." Coltrane took a quick step to the main instigator and grabbed him by his uniform collar. He held the gun to the man's head as he shoved him to the door. The man called Harley was jostled by his friend.

His sidearm still pointed at the perpetrator's head, Coltrane yanked the soldier around to face him and flung the door wider before he kicked him where it would hurt most.

The soldier doubled over as Coltrane thrust them both out, one falling on top of the other. He stood in the doorway, glanced down at them as they gathered themselves in the dust and stumbled toward their horses.

"I ever find you here again, or hear about you coming back, you won't be leaving alive." He stood and watched as they mounted and rode off before he clicked the door shut and holstered his gun. He twisted toward her.

"I should've shot those bastards. Men like that'll be back. They always come back."

She took a deep breath, tension tightened her shoulders, her blood tingled in her veins. "No. Your threat to tell their commanding officer—"

"They know damn well their commander won't give a damn. And we only have the name Harley."

"That's enough to go on. I'll go." But she figured she mightn't. Going to the fort to complain was like walking into a snake pit to ask them not to bite. And one glance at Coltrane told her he didn't believe her either.

"They'll be back," he repeated. "And next time I *will* kill them."

****

Their dinner was solemn, pensive, quiet. Only the occasional clatter of a utensil broke the silence, or Shiloh clearing his throat, stealing glances at her. The doctor kept her gaze on her plate, asked quietly if he wanted more.

"No, thanks, that was more than I've had for a meal in a long time. Bones is a good cook, but not this good." He gave her one of his slight smiles before he scraped his chair back. "You know I won't be leaving here tonight. Not tonight. And I'm worried 'bout you living out here on your own. For sure as night follows day, they'll be back."

"If so, next time I'll be more careful who I open my door to. And I have the knife."

He breathed out heavily. He was totally torn up inside. He didn't feel he could leave her out here alone but knew he had to. Not only would she not let him stay permanently, but he had a ranch to see to, chores to do, and his sister's killers still on the loose. "You know how to use a gun?"

"Of course."

"Then don't hesitate to use it next time and keep it to hand always. Better than the knife. Don't open that door without it by you, don't be outside without it on your hip."

She snickered. "I don't wear a holster, Mr. Coltrane."

"Don't you think it's time you called me Shiloh? I'm spending the night here."

The set of her shoulders told him he wouldn't get farther than the front room floor.

"Anyway," he continued, "you best be buying a holster and keep that gun at your side. You're asking for trouble out here on your own. Really."

"And as I've said before, it's *really* none of your concern." She rose from the table and snatched up the dishes, headed to the wash pan, and put a kettle on to heat the water.

He gazed at her, the slim figure, the golden hair, that tiny waist he'd like to wrap his hands around, pull her back into his arms, nuzzle her neck. That was probably what married couples did, aside from the bedroom stuff. Affection. Togetherness. Love. It suddenly struck him what she must really be like, what he didn't know about her, what made her become a doctor, what her past was.

"Unusual for a woman to choose to be a doctor."

She stopped what she was doing for a moment, her arms rigid by her side. Then she lifted the kettle and poured the hot water.

"Here, let me wash." He rose from his chair and

shunted it back under the table.

"You didn't complain when I treated you."

He took the scrub brush from her, and she picked up the cloth to dry.

"I'm not complaining. Did I complain? I just wanted to know what made you choose to follow this path. You said, I recall, your parents didn't approve."

"No, they didn't. I'm not sure how I got interested in medicine. I just always felt there was something more to life than just being some man's…some man's servant, if you will. Do the cooking, cleaning, or run the household, and bring up children, and that's all. I don't find that idea particularly appealing."

"You don't want children?" It disappointed him, that answer, though he wasn't entirely sure why.

She brought her face around to meet his stare, their gazes locking until she spoke. "I'd like children, yes. I didn't mean that. But I don't want to just be some household drudge. I want my own life to live as I see fit, not as some man tells me to."

He considered this, felt the warmth of her body as they stood side by side. He couldn't stop his thought, help but wonder what it would be like to be married to a woman like her—no, not *like* her, but to her—far more educated than he, independent as she was, opinionated. He'd never thought of marriage before; his life hadn't suited it. But now he had the ranch. Once he'd done what he knew he must, he could settle. That would ease his mind, finding those killers. He'd be real easy in his mind then.

****

Sydney watched as he rolled out his bedroll where the table had been, now pushed aside. "I'll get you some fresh water," she said as she made a move toward the door.

"No. You don't know who might be lurking out there, who might've snuck up. I'll go."

Frustrated, she stamped her foot. "You are *sooo* annoying! You won't be here tomorrow night, or the night after. I look after myself, Mr. Coltrane! I—"

"I thought we were using first names now." His hands found his hips, and he had that funny smile once more.

She pursed her lips, tried to hold in her anger. "It doesn't matter what I call you! You are still the most infuriating man I've ever met."

"Met many, then?" He had one brow up and a smirk now.

"I'm a doctor. Of course I've 'met' many."

"Dead or alive?"

"Very funny." She grabbed the dishcloth and flicked it before spreading it out on the handle of the range. "Good night!"

"Good night, Sydney," he said mildly as she headed for her bedroom and slammed the door.

In the dark, she lay as she did many nights, the moon glowing through her window, a shadow cast of the cross panes, her thoughts simmering in her brain. He had asked why she had become a doctor, and her answer had not been the complete truth. She recalled now a dinner party her parents had given when she was sixteen, new acquaintances her father had met at his bank—a professor and his wife. Sydney had formed an instant attachment to them, held the woman in high esteem, admired her greatly for being a doctor, having a profession. And the husband! It had been love at first sight, or what she considered love at her tender age, a crush, infatuation of the deepest variety. Not only had he been kind, handsome, and good-natured, unlike the example her own father had set, but he was learned and interesting, fascinating even. She would have walked over freshly fired nails had he asked her. The example they had set stayed with her. She would emulate them, walk the same path as they.

From the front room came the sound of the board creaking as Shiloh turned in his sleep. A very different man from Professor Willis. A man who took things into his own hands, a man of doing, of action rather than study, complacency, and thought. There was something here that attracted her as well. There was kindness in Coltrane, but kindness of a different sort, and where the professor had been handsome with his goatee, dark eyes, and studious, respectable demeanor, Shiloh Coltrane had a sort of rough-and-ready beauty to him, the unkempt appearance and bearing of someone who worked hard to get what he wanted. That, too, was very appealing.

Her loneliness grew on her, was amplified with the knowledge there was a man in the next room whose soft, even breathing she imagined she could hear. Other things she could imagine, too. Sleeping in his arms, his hard body wrapped around her, their legs entwined, the intimacy of shared jokes, little whispers through the soft night. And if she went through that door? If she lay down next to him?

If she could just have the peace of companionship for one night?

Her bed moaned slightly as she shifted her weight to touch her bare feet to the floor; her light nightdress fell about her. Cat-like, she tiptoed and clasped the doorknob, stopped in her tracks, wondered if she knew what she was doing, and why she was doing it. Just a peek, she told herself. Just a glance to let her imagination know better. A kind of yearning and curiosity rolled into one.

Giving in to her own inability to sleep unless she just had this one glimpse of him, she turned the knob and slipped into the front room. The profile of Shiloh bundled in his bedroll, lit by the moon, greeted her. She advanced with care, afraid to wake him, and then heard the metallic clunk as his gun hit the floor. She stood and stared down at him: his hands cradled his head, elbows akimbo, the thin smile upon his lips.

And then he reached out his hand, his palm open, and she let the long fingers wrap around her wrist and guide her down.

Shiloh threw back the cover for her to slip in beside him. He knew very well she hadn't come for what he wanted. There would be none of that tonight. And he would let her take the lead. Somehow, he sensed her loneliness was as great as his, but it came from another part of her being. He pulled her in to him, wordless, and wrapped his arms around her, nuzzled into the perfumed scent of her hair. He wanted to tell her not to be afraid, not to fear anything anymore since he'd be there to look after her, but he knew all too well those would be empty words. You can't be there all the time, you can't guard somebody every minute of every day. But when he could, he'd be there for her.

She shifted to face him, their noses practically touching, their mouths a breath away. He still had his arms around her, could feel the swell of her breasts against his chest. If he let his hands roam, he would feel this woman as he had seldom done any woman. Her gaze stayed on his eyes as if she were trying to see into his soul.

At last, she said, "I couldn't sleep. I…"

"Hush now. You don't need an excuse. I'll hold you 'til you do."

He enfolded her tighter, his head now resting in the crux of her neck, so he could hardly hear her say, "Thank you."

In the morning he was gone when she awoke from a deep dreamless sleep. He had carried her to her own bed and covered her up, the bedroll gone and the kitchen table pushed back into place. She had slept through it all, probably felt safe and content in his arms. There was a pot of coffee on the stove and a note scribbled in an almost childish hand, pencil on a scrap of paper taken from the Arbuckle's bag. '*Don't forgit yor gun.*' She looked at it and laughed. So spelling wasn't one of his fortes. But caring was. And he knew how to make coffee.

****

In town, she went into the saloon, her bag heavy but her heart light. The madam greeted her politely as she always did, and followed her up the stairs to the doves' quarters. Each week she interviewed the girls and, if necessary, gave them the colloidal silver thought to be the curative. The conversations weren't always pleasant.

"How are you this week? Any problems?"

The dove slouched back on the couch. "No. Like what?"

"Any bleeding between your menses?"

"My what?"

"Your monthly bleeds. Has there been any bleeding after your intimate encounters or when there otherwise should not have been?"

The woman sat up. "My 'intimate encounters' have been just fine. What are you saying?"

"I'm asking if you are well. Is there any pain during your sexual encounters or urination?"

"During what?"

The madam pulled at her own décolletage. "Oh, come on, Pet. I don't want this to take all day. Behave, for chrissake. Is it painful to piss?"

"No, why should it be?"

Sydney took a deep breath. The last question was not going to go down any easier. "Have you any discharge you've noticed?" She tried to make it more comprehensible to the dove. "From between your legs."

"Discharge?" The dove looked around as if to bring her co-workers in on the joke. "I discharge regularly. I discharge the damned prick when he's through."

Sydney sat back and took a breath. The smell of cheap perfume and sweat hung in the air like pollen on a humid summer's day. "Fine. If you feel at all unwell ask...ask Madam Collette to get hold of me, please. Next!"

When she had finished interviewing all the women, Madam Collette followed her out onto the landing and dropped a quarter-eagle into her hand.

"I've heard talk," she said. "There are men who don't respect a woman living on her own. You mind yourself now, you hear?"

"I've already had a visit, but thank you for the

warning."

"You've had a visit and lived to tell the tale?"

Sydney pondered whether to be forthright with her, then decided it might be best if word was to get around. "Shiloh Coltrane took care of them."

"He *killed* them?"

"Why, no. He scared them off."

"Well, what in the name of... Listen to me, sweetheart. You don't want nothing to do with Shiloh Coltrane. He's a killer. You're a huckleberry above a persimmon around here, and Shiloh's not the man for you."

"I didn't say... He just happened to be there at the right time." Sydney's gaze swept the barroom below. Her heart was pounding in the hope he might be downstairs.

Instead, the one man she spotted was Harley.

"I...I didn't think soldiers were allowed in here."

"Maybe not, but that's their business, not mine. If they're paying, they can drink. The Army don't run the saloon."

Sydney could feel the blood leave her face. In her hand, her bag felt like dead weight. "I...Can I use the back stairs, please? I'd rather not go through the barroom."

Madam Collette's gaze shifted from Sydney to the room below and back again. "One of them there then? And no Shiloh Coltrane to protect you."

"It's fine, though. I'll be fine." But in her head she heard the warning.

Chapter Five

She'd been to the fort only a couple of times before, once to confer professionally with the doctor there, whose pomposity astounded her and who she found had little respect for her as a professional. The other time was to complain about missing items from the provisions shipment they had delivered to the reservation, and that certainly did no good. Phrases like, "Are you accusing us of stealing?" showed no endearment on either side of the confrontation.

Now she had to accuse two soldiers of attacking her and, before she even opened her mouth, knew it would not meet a sympathetic ear.

As her horse splashed across the river and she passed the small Indian scouts' encampment, the doors to the fort swung open. They must have been watching her for a time, knew who she was. She rode past the provost marshal's quarters and then the officers' quarters before trotting through the parade ground, empty at the moment. Dismounting in front of headquarters, all eyes upon her there, she tied her horse to a rail. A silence met her—men stopped what they were doing and stared. Sydney felt as if she were being eaten alive.

She walked up to the offices, felt the piercing glances as she knocked once before entering.

The company clerk, an ugly squat man with some

pustular skin condition and greased-back dirty hair, stared up at her. Sydney could smell him as she opened the door.

"Can I help you?"

"I've come for a word with Colonel Wright."

"And it concerns…?"

"I think I'll wait to see the colonel, if you don't mind."

"You may have to wait a long time unless it's urgent."

She stared at the horrid man a moment and shook her head. "Can you tell him I'm here, please."

The clerk returned her stare as if it were a game to see who gave up first, then arose from his chair. "Have a seat, miss. I'll see what I can do."

"It's Doctor, as well you know."

The clerk ignored her and opened the door into the inner office. There was a muffled exchange before he came back out. "He's engaged at the moment. If you care to have a seat…?"

Sydney plunked herself down on one of the benches and tried to be calm. It wasn't easy, knowing there might be patients who waited to see her, but she also knew she couldn't live her life fearful of who was around the next corner, nor dependent on Shiloh Coltrane for help. Reporting the men was the only way. Having them punished.

What seemed like an interminable hour must have passed by the time the colonel finally opened the door. "Miss Cantrell. So good to see you once again." Sarcasm dripped from him.

She decided it might be best to ignore the 'miss' and just say what she had come to say.

He ushered her into his office and motioned to a chair on the other side of his desk from where he seated himself. "What can I do for you today? Surely no more missing items from your provisions."

Confronted with the situation, she now wasn't sure how to begin. She hesitated until the colonel lifted his brows in question. "I was visited a few nights ago by two of your men. And it wasn't a courtesy call, nor for tea, Colonel."

"I doubt they were from the fort. If any man paid a call on you, Miss Cantrell—"

She gave up her reluctance to irritate him. He was irritating her, so she stood her ground. "Actually, Colonel Wright, I believe you're aware it's *Doctor* Cantrell."

"Ah, yes. You have said before. Some degree from a women's college or other. Well, as you like, *Doctor.*"

Her hands were in her lap. Anger mixed with nervousness as she knew the outcome of this meeting would bring no resolution. Her palms felt cold and clammy. Still, she must speak her piece. She waited for her head to clear. "Colonel Wright, have you got a soldier named Harley?"

His gaze burned into her with distaste. Cornered. "John Harley, yes."

"And how do you think I would know the man's name if I hadn't heard him called that in front of me? Aside from the fact both men were in uniform."

"I have no idea, Miss…Doctor Cantrell. You could have heard it out on the street for all I know." He leaned back, his fingers arching together, tips tapping.

"Harley and another man came to my cabin pretending to be in need of medical attention. They forced their way in, grabbed me from behind, made insinuations of what they would like to do with me—and I think you know very well what I mean—and almost succeeded. The other man, whose name I do not know, wanted Harley to clear the table to proceed."

"But you somehow succeeded in stopping them?" The colonel glanced out the window before turning back to her. "I find this very difficult to believe, Doctor. If two men attacked me, I doubt very much I would be able to overcome them alone."

Her voice now rose. "It doesn't matter how I was able to overcome them, Colonel. Their intentions were clear, and I got them to leave. I just saw Harley drinking in one of the town's saloons, something I imagine is forbidden by the Army?"

"Ah! I see. You were in the saloon."

"Yes, I was. I'm doctor to the unfortunate girls there—if you don't mind. As I am doctor to your laundresses here, who come to see me when they can." She tried to hide the smirk she felt.

Colonel Wright tapped the desk. "Well, it is all very unfortunate, Doctor. I really am quite sorry for your…your inconvenience. I can hardly be expected to watch each and every man in this fort at all times, and I have no proof as to what they did other than your word. I'm afraid it's not enough to go on."

"What sort of proof would you like, Colonel? A dead body with an Army revolver lying conveniently by its side?"

The colonel continued to tap the table for another minute, his gaze studying her as if he were committing her features to memory. He rose. "I think we're finished here today, Doctor Cantrell. I'll keep in mind what you said, and if I see any reason for suspicion other than what you have told me, I will certainly investigate. But the word of a single woman is hardly anything to go on." His arm extended as if pointing to the door.

She rose and gave him one long look.

Colonel Wright jerked open the door. "Sergeant Parmeter, Miss Cantrell is just leaving."

For a moment Sydney froze. Her gaze met the oily visage of the company clerk before she marched out the door and slammed it behind her.

Through the afternoon, she seemed to be treating her patients as if she were some sort of automated being. Her mind could not leave Parmeter now. Who in heaven's name was at that fort? First, the two men who had attacked her, now Parmeter, whom Shiloh had said had been married to his sister. Oswald Parmeter, if she remembered correctly. If it were the same man. By the look of the clerk, it could well be, though she knew she shouldn't be judging this person on his looks. Then again, how many Parmeters could there be swanning about in the area?

And should she tell Shiloh? That was the big question.

If she told him, he would be sure to fly off and confront the man, probably gun him down. That was obvious from what he had said, from what Madam Collette had divulged. "He's a killer." She went through the things he himself had related. "I've killed men and will kill more." She couldn't understand how a man who had been so gentle and caring with her could go off and take a life. Would he even try to bring those murderers in for the law to deal with? No, he had already said he wouldn't. He didn't trust the law, the jails, the system.

And yet she felt he had a right to know and make the decision for himself. But not yet. Not while she wasn't sure. And if it was Oswald Parmeter, and Shiloh did kill him, what then? What would she feel? Would she feel guilt at having told him? Or would she just feel…what? The loss of someone she cared about because he had done this terrible thing. No longer able to meet his glances, speak with him. What then?

****

Shiloh sat at his kitchen table, a torn latigo in his hands, the saddle beside it, and tried to figure the easiest way to mend it. But his mind wasn't on latigos—it was on hyacinth eyes and hair like spun gold and the warmth of that woman in his arms all night. Someone had once told him opposites attract, and he had to wonder if it were true, if she had any feeling for him whatsoever. He suspected she did; why else would she sleep beside him all night like that? Yet she was tough and independent, and he knew she didn't approve of his past—she had made that clear. Still, he could always hope. Once he had dealt with his sister's and nephew's killers, he could think about making this a real home for himself.

"You were turning that round in your hands the last time I come in." Bones stepped through the doorway and shook his head. "You day-dreamin' somethin' awful. That's a sure way for accidents to happen."

Shiloh didn't look at him. He kept twisting the latigo in his hands. "What accident do you think is going to happen, me sitting here and all. Doing nothing."

"Well, now. Accidental heartbreak is what I think

is gonna happen. You dwellin' on that woman, and you know dang well she ain't no one for you. Why, she so far off the mark—"

"All right. I've got it." He dropped the latigo and stood with such force his chair toppled over. As he bent to right it, his gaze met Bones'. "You think I don't know all that? But how do you know she hasn't taken a liking to me? How do you know she's not sitting out there lonely and wishing I'd come?"

Bones shook his head again and headed toward the cook stove. "She too sensible for that." He started to measure out some grounds for fresh coffee. "You think she gonna tie up with a killer…"

"I'm not a killer anymore. Or at least won't be once I finish with Parmeter and his friends."

"Yeah. And that's a real comfort to her, I s'ppose. She gonna feel real safe 'round you."

"She'd be a helluva lot safer around me than she is right now." Shiloh grabbed his hat off a peg and headed to the door. "At least I could look after her."

****

Indian Paintbrush and Blazing Star. He stopped to pick some wildflowers on his ride over. She'd like that. It would brighten her day, maybe make her a bit less serious. Make him seem less like some hard-bitten killer. It made him feel silly, boyish, but the thought she'd appreciate the flowers also made him smile.

As he rode up to her cabin, he knew she wasn't in. There was no light, and no horse in the corral. He dismounted and loosened the cinch on his own horse, tied him to the rail. For a moment, he was unsure as to whether he should enter her home without being asked, but the thought of the flowers wilting or dying without her seeing them didn't strike him as sensible.

The cabin was as he remembered it. Tidy, clean, spare. He strode over to the bedroom and peeked in. That too was barren. A bed. A side table, and one more table with her wash basin and pitcher. A hand mirror. A brush. A lantern. He could offer her so much more, give her a better life.

From outside he heard his horse whinny.

The flowers were still in his hand as he returned to the kitchen and tossed his hat on the table. He glanced around for something to put the wildflowers in. There was only the pitcher, so that would have to do, even if she might need it later. It had some standing water in it, and he plunked the flowers in as the door opened.

Sydney stood stock still, her face expressionless. Without ceremony she demanded, "What are you doing?"

He gazed across at her, his small smile stretching his lips. "Thought you might like these."

"You have no right! You have no right to just come in and make yourself at home. How dare you!"

He blinked as he thought this through. "I rode over to see how you were doing, picked you some flowers, and then found you weren't in. What was I supposed to do? Just throw them away? Leave them on your doorstep?" He waited. "This is the west. It's called hospitality of the west. People leave their doors open. Other people can come in if they need to." He set the pitcher on the table. "You saw my horse, knew it was me, I take it."

She moved past him and dropped her bag on the table. "Leaving the flowers outside might have been better than coming in without asking, without my permission. Just because…just because…"

But he didn't let her finish. He couldn't help himself, couldn't stop himself any longer. In one quick stride, he had cupped her chin and lifted her face so their gazes locked and his mouth was on hers. At first, stunned, Sydney hit him with her fists, but it was merely seconds before she succumbed and let his kiss go deeper, melted into him as if her body was meant to be blended with his, as if her yearning and her need were as great as his.

Breathless, she covered his hands with her own and gently released herself, held his hands before she twisted away.

"Don't." She put her hand to her forehead as if contemplating what to do next, then gripped the back of one of the chairs at the table.

He came up behind her. "You going to tell me not to, you can't, you have no feelings for me?"

"No."

"What then?"

"It…it won't work, Shiloh. We're too different, we're poles apart—"

"Because of my past?"

She took a deep breath and faced him. "That's something to do with it. But—"

He leaned against the far wall studying her. "So you think I should just leave things be, let my sister and her little boy's killers go free, walk around, leave it to the law to find them."

"Yes, leave it to the law."

"Well let me tell you something, lady. The marshal came down here, took a few notes on the case, and left. That's how much interest he had in it. No one cares a dang fig about what happened. No one is going to solve it because there's not enough to go on at the moment."

Sydney flinched.

"I, myself, haven't got a clue where to start. But someday something is going to turn up, and I'm going to act upon it. And if you think the decent thing is for me to just turn a blind eye and let it be, then you're wrong. You may think it's right to just go on healing people no matter what they've done—"

"I never said that! I would do what I could so they would face trial, but I would bring them to justice."

"There's no justice here, Sydney. There's just the law folks can take into their own hands." He paced a few steps, the sudden silence heavy like a storm brewing. "You may think this is some bright new world and we're soon to face a whole new century, but things in Wyoming haven't changed all that much. Why, it's just a few years back since the trouble over in Johnson County. You think folks have changed overnight?"

"No. But I do think the change has to start somewhere. With decent people. Setting an example…"

"Bringing your civilization from back east?"

"If you want to put it that way, then yes."

He strolled over to the window and peered out, his head tilted in thought. He pivoted back to her. The setting sun cast his shadow along the floorboards, and the room suddenly seemed dark and somber.

"I can't change myself. I have feelings for you, and I think you have feelings for me."

Sydney seemed to shake, as if she had a sudden chill. Or someone had stepped on her grave.

"But I can't change myself. I can't let those deaths go unpunished. That's my flesh and blood, and even if it weren't..." He strolled back to her, easing something out of his back pocket. "My sister sent me this photo taken on her wedding day some years back. This is a person, see, another woman, my sister, and I need to make amends for not protecting her, not being there when she needed me." He held out the photo and thought Sydney looked at it almost reluctantly, her face going white as she did. "So now you see? Now you know."

He slipped the photograph back into his pocket, picked up his hat and set it on his head, never taking his gaze from her. His voice was low when he said, "I'm falling in love with you, but I'm willing to have you the way you are—your beliefs, your work, your views of how things should be. I wish I thought you felt the same about me."

Sydney stood in the darkening room for a time after she heard the hoofbeats die away. It *was* the same Parmeter, there was no doubt about it. And there was no doubt about what Shiloh would do if she told him. She needed to save Shiloh from himself; he would get himself hanged or killed in his efforts to right a wrong and bring his own brand of justice to this man.

She slumped into a kitchen chair, her head in her hands. As she moved, the letter she had collected from the post office that morning crinkled in her skirt pocket, and she slid it out, unfolded it with care. The familiar hand, neat and even, cultured, learned, greeted her with its flowing script—such a contrast to the printed misspelled words written by Shiloh the other day.

31 August 1899

My dearest Sydney,

It has been some time since I have heard from you,

and I yearn for word of how you are faring out in the untamed Wyoming wilderness. I am hoping your silence is nothing more than a sign of occupation, that the Indian reservation you described and the local townspeople are keeping you busy. Your last letter was so full of joy at being there, I felt surely you must have little time to spare for writing to this old widower.

My classes at the university continue much as always. It is difficult for me to be so fully preoccupied with students and books during the day and then return to the deep silence of this huge house. Friends try to take my mind away from my loss, but I cannot discuss with them, I fear, our forthcoming nuptials at this stage. They may look askance at our age difference, perhaps think you are taking advantage of me rather than it being a true love match.

I know we agreed a year's separation before said nuptials would take place, thus giving me the correct time for bereavement before taking on a new life with you, and giving you a year of independence and adventure before being tied to staid Philadelphia and perhaps less interesting patients. However, if you find it in your heart to return early to me, I am sure we could together face our colleagues and these challenges, and in time, they would accept the situation.

Let me know if there is any hope of this.
Your loving mentor and faithful friend,
Garnforth A. Willis, MD

Chapter Six

Her dreams were so real, she periodically woke in the night, sweating first, then chilled, dazed. Each time she would look at her watch brooch by the bedside and be surprised at how little time had passed since the last awakening. Sips of water and sitting up to clear her head did no good. As soon as she fell back to sleep, the dreams would start again—patients lined up outside her cabin, turning to her, arms reaching out, their faces going black in front of her. Parmeter laughing as he sliced off Shiloh's arm. The saloon girls, all laughing in a circle. One after another, the dreams tormented her through the night until daybreak, when she was thankful for this anguish to be over, however little sleep she got.

The flowers on the table were a reminder of the decision she faced. She stood over them a moment recalling Shiloh's kiss, the feel of his arms around her that night she slept beside him, his small smile that altered his face, and her surprise at his graceful hands. She knew she would never feel about Garnforth the way she felt about Shiloh, the professor would never stir inside her the emotions and longings Shiloh Coltrane moved within her. Her relationship with the professor would be a meeting of like minds, quiet comfort in companionship, a steadiness and routine of predictability. But was that what she wanted?

Shiloh's kiss had left her wanting more, wanting him, but was that wise?

As she saddled her horse, she realized she had a choice to make: tell Shiloh or tell Parmeter. If she told Shiloh, he would kill the other man surely, and get himself arrested and probably hanged in the process. She believed there was little proof as to Parmeter's involvement other than Shiloh's word. If she told Parmeter, he would most likely leave, knowing Shiloh was on his trail. Halfway to the reservation she made up her mind and took the fork in the road that led to the fort.

The gates swung open once again, and she skirted around the parade ground as soldiers stood out for inspection. She hesitated only a moment before dismounting at the headquarters and tying up her horse, then climbing the steps to the office.

Parmeter looked up in surprise at her entry, no doubt because of her swift return after the other day. She stood before him as he ran a hand through his greasy hair, and his eyes widened in question.

"You're back. What is it this time?"

"Oswald Parmeter?"

The clerk looked wary, uncertain at the inclusion of his first name. "What do you want?" It came as a snarl.

"I know who you are. I'll be reporting you to the sheriff in town, and—"

"Report? Report for what? Report away. I'm under Army law; the sheriff has no jurisdiction here. And what is it you think I have done?"

"You were married to Shiloh Coltrane's sister. You were involved in her murder."

The door from the colonel's office swung open.

The colonel glanced from Parmeter to Sydney and back again. "What is going on here?"

Parmeter rose from his seat. "The good doctor seems to be delusional, sir. She seems to think I am someone else."

She slammed the desk, her face contorted. "I am warning you to get out. Shiloh will be after you as soon as I tell him where you are!"

"You see, sir." Parmeter turned his slimy smile to the colonel. "She thinks I am someone else."

"He's a murderer! He either killed his wife or had her killed—she was killed because of his mixing with outlaws!"

"What wife? I have no wife, miss. You mistake me for someone else."

"Colonel, I am telling you—this man is a murderer."

The colonel looked from one to the other, uncertainty and doubt coloring his anger. "I think you better go, Doctor. Perhaps living out here has somehow affected your thinking. Parmeter has been with me for some time now—"

"Some time? A year or so?"

"What difference does it make? I have no complaints against this man."

"So you are happy to continue with him as company clerk if he is a murderer?"

The colonel sighed. "Doctor Cantrell. Please leave this fort now and do not return unless you have firm proof of some wrongdoing."

She held her stance for a moment, her gaze shifting from one to the other. What had she been thinking in coming here? What in heaven's name had she hoped to accomplish? *Saving Shiloh from himself?* Maybe he was right—the only law in Wyoming was the law you created yourself or left to men like him. It was obvious now what her next step must be.

Shiloh would have to know, and he would have to know soon.

****

He couldn't get her off his mind. There'd been women in his life, temporary associations, affairs on the run, moments of comfort and release. But no one had ever stirred within him the feelings Sydney brought on. Her goodness and her care were overpowering addictions, an attraction for which he had no precedent. Perhaps it was time to settle down, make a home here— yet always in the back of his mind were his sister's and nephew's deaths. He knew he would never rest easy until they were avenged, until their killers had been found. He would always be on the lookout, always be wondering, forever have that space in his mind and heart that said he should find those men, whatever the cost.

Bones caught his eye, riding the other side of the herd as they gathered them in to bring to lower ground. He gave a small nod in the direction of Shiloh's left, and before he even swung that way, he knew what he would see. Sydney was riding hard, her hat low on her brow, the stampede string pulled tight to her jaw as she reined up.

Surprise must have been written on his face because in the moment she caught her breath the shadow of a smile appeared so fleetingly on her face, it was gone long before she could speak.

"Well, what are you—?"

"Parmeter," she breathed. "He's clerk to the colonel at the fort. In headquarters."

He sat back in his saddle, the reins loose in his hand as he gaped at her, his mouth dry as the words took their time. "You're sure?" he finally got out.

"I heard the colonel address him. Then you showed me the photograph. It confirmed my suspicion."

"When...why didn't you tell me sooner? Tell me when you saw the photograph?"

Sydney seemed to squirm, then tapped her hat as she gathered herself. "I confronted him. I—"

"You confronted him! Are you stark raving mad?" His anger rose like a storm on a summer's day. "You've put yourself at risk! And you've given him warning?"

"I...I don't want you getting hurt. I thought if I told him, he'd...he'd turn himself in, or the Army would do something. Rather than you getting yourself killed or hanged!"

"That wasn't your decision to make!"

"I was trying to save you!"

"Save me? From what? You know now what they'll do? They'll either run or come after you before you can further stir up things for them. Or both. This gives me little time, Sydney. Little time to plan!"

"Plan what, for goodness sake? Plan to kill them?"

"Yes!" He waited for her response, but there was none. "I've told you all along I would go after them as soon as I found them. I'm not going to let them be, let them get away with what they did."

"No, you'd rather get yourself killed than leave it to the law, wouldn't you?" She was leaning over the pommel, her face reddening with her anger.

"If I have to, yes! I'll die avenging my family's deaths."

"Then all those fine words about your feelings for me amount to nothing. If you're dead, what difference do they make, Shiloh? Tell me that."

He let out a long breath, his gaze fixed on her. "I told you I wanted you just the way you are and hoped you would want me the way I am. That's what I said. You can't go around trying to change me, protect me from myself, Sydney. I am what I am. And I said this would be the end, the last time I would kill would be when I found my family's murderers."

"The trouble is, Shiloh, you say that now, but there's always one more. Always one more death to avenge, one more wrong to right. It's in your nature. And it's in mine to…to try to stop it. So I guess we're just not meant to be." She sat back, calmer now. "I don't know what we're discussing here. We hardly know each other. Somehow you've decided you have feelings for me."

He laughed, a harsh guffaw. "I've decided? You think I don't know what my feelings are? Every time I think of you my heart pounds, the blood runs jittery in my veins. I can't wait to see you again. I think of you all day until I forget what I'm doing."

Sydney stared blindly at him, her mind somewhere else, as if she were seeing something for the first time, something only in her head but clear to her as day. A magpie flew up suddenly from the brush, and its caw brought her back to the moment.

He sat and gazed at her, wanting her so much he thought his heart beat loud enough for her to hear it. It seemed to him several minutes passed in which the silence between them said more than their words.

"I wanted to court you," he said at last. "I wanted to do things properly. I can offer you a good home here on the ranch—it's making fair money. It's comfortable now, but you could do as you liked with it, fix it to your liking. Maybe it's not what you had in mind, but the cabin you're living in is—"

"Shiloh, I'm a doctor. I told you I'm not going to be some—"

"That's just it, Sydney. I said I don't want to change you, and I meant it. You could work if that's what you want."

"But you're still going after those men."

"Yes."

"Then I'm sorry. I'm sorry about a lot of things, but mostly I'm sorry about the loss of you as a friend."

Seeing Sydney ride away put an emptiness in him, a bruise on his heart, a loneliness deeper than any he had felt before and that he knew couldn't be healed. For a while he sat there. His mind turned, tried to get hold of what was more important to him—revenging his sister's and nephew's deaths or having Sydney, or at least seeing if they could work it out, courting her, loving her. Were the living more important than the dead, or wasn't that part of the question? It seemed he couldn't do both.

He was taken from these deliberations by Bones loping up. The old man sat his horse, fingers tapping the pommel, reins sagging from his hand as his horse took the opportunity to crop pasture. For several moments there was no other sound than the grass yanked from its roots, the occasional low of the cattle, and the susurration of the wind. He knew Bones had infinite patience, and he knew what the old cowboy wanted to know.

"She's found Parmeter. Says he's over at the fort, company clerk or some such. Warned him to get out, that I would come for him."

Bones sat back, easy in his saddle but a look of incredulity on his face. "Thought she be smarter than that. What she go and do that for?"

"To save me, apparently." He took a deep breath and adjusted his hat. "Now she's in danger, and the bastard knows I'm coming for him."

"Well, you better be quick as all-get-out, 'cause you know for sure now they gonna come get her before she stirs anything more. That was one pretty dang stupid thing to do."

"Yeah." Shiloh gazed off into the distance, pondering his situation. "Yeah, that was not smart. I better get off back to the house and load up. Don't know when I'll be back. Can you—"

"You goin' for her, or you goin' for them? 'Cause you know she needs protectin' now."

"I'm going for them, Bones. That's the only way I can protect her, even if she's not going to be happy about it. I sat here and considered it all, whether I should just let things be. But I can't. I'll never rest easy 'til those men are dead, and now I have an even stronger reason to get them." He shook his head in resolve. "You think you can manage, then? Maybe get Bates to help, tell him I'll pay a good wage or help in return."

"Jus' you make sure you come on back to pay him, then."

Shiloh gathered his reins. "If I don't return, the

place is yours."

****

Bozy looked at the money laid out on the bar counter, then back up at Shiloh. "That's more than the window's worth. Especially if you'll be fixing it for me."

"Information. And if I live to fix it, it'll be done, but for now, information."

The bartender looked suspicious. He squinted at the coins, then back up at Shiloh. "What sort of information? You not going on about that same gang who killed your sister and her son? Told you all I knew." He moved two of the coins back toward Shiloh. "Here you take that, and stop asking questions. Not gonna do you any good, nor me."

"Some of the soldiers drink here on occasion. I've seen them. Not good for them nor for you, Bozy."

"What about it? What business is it of yours? I'm not their keeper!" His truculence rose fast. "If they pay, they're welcome to drink. Let their commanding officers penalize them or whatever."

"Parmeter. Parmeter is the company clerk, I hear. My sister's husband. Does he come in?"

"I don't know. I don't know any of them by name. I serve them and collect the money. That's it, Shi—"

But he wasn't having that for an answer. He reached across and got Bozy by his shirt collar and pulled him halfway across the bar.

The saloon fell silent.

"I asked you a question. A civil question, for which information I am willing to pay."

The bartender's voice came as a croak. "All right. Let me down!"

Shiloh eased off and let the man's feet hit the floor. "It's all right, folks," he said in a louder voice as he twisted toward the other drinkers. "Slight misunderstanding." In a low voice to Bozy, the single name: "Parmeter."

Bozy straightened himself out, pulled his shirt down, and dusted at himself as if Shiloh had dirtied him. "Company clerk, from what I know."

"That much I've heard."

"Comes in and seems to meet up with about four other guys occasionally."

"Names?"

"Dunno. One of 'em's a big fat guy. Seen him ride a huge roan. Others I can't really describe. They always got their hats pulled down low as if they don't want to be recognized. All pretty much the same, medium build, medium height. But nasty. Snarly. Rough with the girls. You ask Collette, she'll tell you. She says she can do without their custom. One, I think, comes in alone, maybe from Colorado, not sure. You hear bits and can't always piece them together."

Shiloh grimaced, sick with himself he'd never noticed these men. Then again, he was rarely in town. Now he didn't like to think about what they did to his sister, nor more especially what they might do to Sydney. "Do they name any place they came from? Any jobs they've done? Surely you must've picked up something."

"I'm telling you, Coltrane. I don't like having them here and neither does anyone else. Other customers finish their drinks and leave when those men come in. There's a sense of trouble about them, and I stay outa their way and hope they're gone quick."

"And are they?"

"Not so's I see. They take their time, as if they haven't a care in the world. As if they own the place. Parmeter's often the first to go, throws a few coins on the table and leaves for the fort. The others generally avail themselves of Madam Collette's ladies. Then they go."

"Do you at least see which way they ride out?"

"Nope. No one way. Sometimes east, sometimes west, sometimes—"

"Yeah, yeah, I get it." He rested an elbow on the bar. He didn't have much more to go on than he'd had before.

"Yeager. There was a man named Yeager once come in asking for Parmeter, said to tell him Yeager was looking for him. Lanky fellow. Dark. Mean-looking, with a scar worse than yours—a knife cut, I'd say. Ran from below his ear and came across his cheek—"

"Yancy Yeager."

"You know him?"

"I rode with him once, much to my regret. Mean son of a gun. Where'd he go?"

"No idea. But the sheriff might know more. Said there's a warrant out for his arrest. Wanted in four states or some such."

"Make that five." He pushed the coins over to Bozy. "I'll be back to do the window."

"Maybe you better do it before you find Parmeter and Yeager," Bozy called after him.

But the swing of the saloon doors was his only answer.

****

79

Sheriff Barnes was none too happy to see Shiloh Coltrane walk through his door, and he didn't hesitate to let the gunman know. Wiry and old, Barnes was aware of Shiloh's reputation, as the younger man well knew. But there were no Wanted posters out on him, sitting there in a stack on the sheriff's desk. He had no reason to fear going into the sheriff's office, and the sheriff had no reason to turn him away.

Barnes sat back and rocked a bit, his feet up on his desk, his fingers arched in a cathedral of straw-colored skin. His pale face crumpled like old paper.

"What do you want, Coltrane? You bounty-hunting now?"

"Sheriff, I don't know why you dislike me so, and I have no idea what would give you that idea."

"Humph." Barnes stomped his feet down and bent forward; the gnarled fingers gripped the edge of his desk. "So to what do I owe the pleasure?"

"Yancy Yeager. He's been in town, I hear. I want to know where he's gone."

"You sure do like to look for trouble."

"I believe he's one of the men who killed my sister and her son. I didn't ask for this job, but it seems since you haven't done yours, I'm going to do it for you."

The sheriff narrowed his eyes, his finger like the branch of an ancient wind-bent tree pointing at Shiloh. "Now you listen here, son. I went after those men we thought killed your family. And I rode for several days without luck. Where were you then, huh? You tell me that."

"That's months ago now, Sheriff. You gave up rather quickly."

"And I never saw you take my place. You came in

here, asked a few questions, and left it."

"More to my shame. But your answers, as I recall, didn't tell me very much to go on. What was I supposed to do? Ride the entire West looking for some unknown gang with not a clue to go on? Now I suspect Yeager was one of the men. Or at least I figure so."

"Well, I don't know anything more now."

"I think you do. I hear Yeager's been in town meeting with Parmeter. Right under your nose."

"And right under yours," Sheriff Barnes barked as he leant back again in his chair and let it rock a few beats. "Nothing I can do about Yeager, Coltrane. I haven't seen him, and I'm guessing he hasn't caused any trouble locally."

"Other than killing my family."

"You know that for a fact?"

Shiloh bit his lip. He was back where he was a year ago, uncertain and without proof. "Bozy just told me Yeager is wanted in four states."

"May be, but I don't have the posters or information on that here in Wyoming."

Shiloh didn't believe him but accusing the sheriff wouldn't get him far. *You get more bees with honey.* "Listen. I know you don't like me, and you probably have some good cause. But I'm not going to rest easy until those men are caught. And *that* I think you understand. So just tell me what you know about Yeager, or Parmeter, or both, and anyone else associated with them, and let me handle it my way."

Barnes licked his top lip and sat back for a second, deep in thought. "Yeager was in town last night, then rode out in a hurry. Headed south. I saw Parmeter and the rest of his no-good cohorts all mount up right after, headed in the direction of the fort. Of course Parmeter lives there, but I don't know what the others would be doing—"

But Shiloh knew. He knew all too well.

Chapter Seven

At first, Sydney wasn't sure whether the galloping horses and shouting and laughing she heard was in a dream or real. She struggled to pull herself out of sleep, weary after a long day, confronting Parmeter, informing Shiloh, treating patients. The life split between the reservation, the occasional visits to the fort, and her patients in town or in their homes, wore her out. Groggy, she sat up in bed and listened. Outside. They were outside laughing, the horses whickering and stomping, their hooves knocking the risers of the steps.

Sydney grabbed the handgun beside her bed and tucked her knife into the pocket of her dressing gown as she swung it on to cover herself, just as a torch of lit pitch came crashing through the window of her front room. Her reflex was to scream, but she stopped herself, turned it into a gasp as the cabin took light. There was no time to save her medical bag or anything else. She wheeled toward the back door that led outside to the privy and grabbed the handle.

Jammed. They must have put something there or tied it somehow.

Yanking it proved no good and the flames were beginning to engulf the cabin; medicine bottles popped and exploded, adding fuel to the fire. The sound of shattering glass filled the night.

She took her shotgun by its barrel and smashed the

window behind the bed, knocked out some sharp shards in order to climb through. Still barefoot, she took care to land on the wet grass just as one of the men came around the house and grabbed hold of her gown.

"Now, now, sweetheart, where you think you're goin'?" His voice was oily, gruff, and devious.

Caught in the gown, she got her sidearm into the other hand, shaking violently as she fired blindly. The attacker shouted a resonant curse as he released the cloth and stepped backward toward the cabin, his hand to his chest.

She started running. Running through the trees at the back into the woods. The men shouted and cursed behind her on their horses, taunts of the vilest nature. The pale cloth of the gown served as a marker to them and gave notice as to where she was. Still, breathless, she kept on; the horses stumbled on the damp leaves, through the trees and over the fallen branches. Moonlight cast the sky a pale gray.

She could hear the creak of leather as one of the men dismounted.

And then she was caught.

Another of the men, his breath heavy with drink, his body stinking, flung himself on her from his horse, as the man who held her from behind let her drop. The animal reared and backed off into the woods. Sydney fell with the drunk, the gun lost as he tried to mount her, held her left arm down, her right arm flailing and beating at him. The man who had grabbed her kicked her hand and tried to stomp on it.

Somehow, she managed to scrabble for the knife in her pocket as the two other men stood over the attacker and egged him on, laughing.

"She'll be a pleasure, she will. Doctor! Maybe she can check you afterward, Charley; she'll sure need to check herself."

She released the blade and stuck it in his left side right below the heart; blood spurted and she shoved him away, scrambled from underneath him.

Now one of the others clutched her robe and hauled her to her feet and punched her in the face. "You stupid bitch! Who the hell do you think you are?" It was Parmeter, his voice, his hate. Another punch to her stomach. As she crumpled over, he pulled her up again and gave her a blow to her jaw.

She felt the lost gun by her left foot. She crumpled over to the mossy floor of the woodland, curled as if she were dying, but her hand wrapped around the grip of the gun. Her finger found the action and pulled back the hammer as she raised it and pointed it at her assailant. The sound deafened her for a moment, but she moved the barrel to point at the last man. Shaking and struggling to stay awake, she watched as he backed away, then ran for his horse. She fired once more.

The last thing she heard was the crash as the roof of her cabin fell in.

****

Shiloh left the sheriff knowing he had to get to Sydney's cabin, check on her, see she was all right. He'd barely left town when, in the distance, he could see the figure of a horseman heading in the general direction of his ranch. He knew instantly it was Bones, coming back from the Bates ranch, most likely having asked Bates for help as he had advised. To the west, where Bones rode, was open range, only not so open now, a small buffer between ranches where cattle grazed occasionally. But Shiloh was headed into the woodland, to Sydney's cabin, when he saw Bones pull up and dismount. The old man seemed to be looking at something, searching for something on the ground or at least something held his interest there. He slowed his own horse to observe, but decided getting to Sydney's cabin and getting there fast was more important.

The trouble was, there was no cabin. At first, he thought it was a trick of the growing dark, twilight blindness, but he knew he was kidding himself.

The smell of the fire greeted him long before he galloped in, pulled up to see the rubble that had once been her home. Smoldering and blackened ruins, a pyramid of fallen beams, shattered and melted glass, a bit of what looked like the leather of her medical bag, a shard of the pitcher in which he had put the flowers he'd brought her. Cinders flew about in the wind. The only thing recognizable was her iron bed, collapsed now, the mattress gone, the paint blistered.

Panicking, he dismounted and started to call her name, kicking aside bits of wood, hoisting larger pieces out of his way. He turned sharply as Bones rode in.

"Thought you'd be here. There's tracings of blood on the road to the fort, like someone been shot. You think it's her?'

"They wouldn't dare take her there. She's got to be here somewhere. Got to be."

Bones just shook his head. "Maybe. Maybe not. How many you think there was?"

"Four. I'm almost certain, from things I was told in town. And I'd say the one that went back to the fort would be Parmeter."

"Sister's husband?"

"Yup." Shiloh started to walk around the perimeter of the cabin, shoving other bits with his boot, occasionally lifting items, and throwing them back down. Inside he was sick. He knew what he was going to find but couldn't admit it to himself. He had left things with Parmeter too long, hadn't gone after him and the others when he should have, hadn't got the information out of Bozy soon enough. Now he was going to pay the price with Sydney's life, and he wouldn't be able to live with himself.

Bones bent to move a beam, yanked his hands back from the heat, then kicked aside the rubble. "Well, there's one of 'em. Caught in his own trap!"

Shiloh rushed through to wrench the body out and look at it.

"You recognize him?" Bones stood over his employer as the rancher squatted down to try to see what there might be left of the face.

"Nope." He left the body where it was, other worries on his mind now. The charred body of this killer could rot, for all he cared.

He moved with Bones to the back of the house. He stood and pondered that the fire hadn't gone farther. Obviously, the damp of the leaves had prevented it. A spark had lit the privy and the roof was gone, but that fire had gone out. He stood studying the site, and Bones hollered.

"Look! See that there cloth? Might be a part of a dress or something. Not what a man would wear!"

He hopped over some debris to where Bones was pointing and lifted the fragment.

Sydney's night dress. He was sure. It might not be the same one she wore when she slept in his arms, but he was sure it was hers, a fine dimity, not a man's cloth.

And it was smeared with blood.

His breath was sucked out of him. He felt like his own blood drained from his body and he swayed for a moment. She couldn't be dead. She couldn't be.

"Another one!" Bones shouted. He was squatting by a second body, outside the cabin area, a heavy man whose life had colored his shirt red, bled away. There remained a visage of shock on him, his eyes bulging slightly.

Shiloh skipped over the wreckage to get to him, kneeling down to examine the remains. Bones helped turn the body over so the stab wound was clearly visible.

"She's alive. She must be." He was speaking to himself more than to Bones as he released his grip and the body fell forward once more. "Sydney had a knife. I know that; she showed it to me. She must be hiding, must've got away somehow." As he stood, his heel struck something spongey, something soft. He twisted around.

Another body.

Bones came over and stooped beside him as they examined the wound.

"You think she shot 'im?"

"I told her to get a gun. Maybe she listened and heeded me."

"She a good shot, from what I see. Shot in the stomach. Worst place. No hope. But the other who got away, over yonder, he still losin' blood lessin' he gots help soon enough."

"Or unless it's her." He stood. "Maybe she was coming to us for help." It suddenly struck him. "Her horse is not here."

"Horse woulda run from the fire. No way a horse woulda stuck 'round to see what happen."

"Could have been tied up."

"Coulda. I'll see if there's prints."

"Bones, there won't be, not with this mess." He reached out and rested his hand on the older man's shoulder. It struck him he was comforting himself more than anything else. Someone living and breathing. A friend.

All his years of being mixed up with the wrong people, being a hired gun, the killing had come easy. Until he had to face the fact of having taken someone's life. Even if they deserved it, which in his world they always had. He found it difficult to look upon what had once been living and was now dead. He couldn't think of Sydney that way.

"There's more of that cloth over yonder," Bones said. He pointed to a mass of leaves on the forest floor, the pale dirtied cloth lying there, ruffling a bit in the wind.

But Shiloh saw something more in the moonlight. Mixed in with the ochres and reds and browns of the fallen leaves was a sweep of gold.

Sydney.

He dashed to where she lay, the word "no" going through his brain. *She mustn't be dead, she mustn't be!* He kneeled beside her, hurriedly brushing away the leaves that had blown and covered her, scooping her into his arms. "Sydney? Sydney?"

Bones crouched beside them, tenderly taking one of Sydney's hands and feeling for a pulse, then touching his finger to her neck. There was a slight jerk of her body.

"She alive, Boss. But only just."

"Get my blanket, quick!" He pulled the limp form into his arms to try to warm her. Her face was badly swollen, black and blue, bruises swelling her lips and her eye puffed out. She wouldn't be able to open it. He had seen injuries like these many times, but never on a woman, never on someone he loved. When his sister had been killed, she was long buried by the time he'd got home.

Bones came back with the blanket, shook it out, and laid it on the forest floor as Shiloh bent over and laid Sydney on it. He pulled the two sides together over her and stood with her in his arms.

"You gonna ride with her that way?"

"You'll have to hand her up."

"Where you takin' her, then? She the doc."

"Home. We're going to take her home, Bones." He started to the horses.

"What about these dead?"

"They can rot, for all I care. Maybe you'll go in and tell the sheriff what happened tomorrow, but for now we've got to get Sydney home. Here, take her while I mount up, then you'll have to hand her up to me. I'll get Whiskey over to that stump there; it'll be easier."

"She light as a feather."

Shiloh swung into his saddle and moved his horse so Bones could be level with him before he glided Sydney's inert form into his boss' arms.

"I'll have to go slow. You ride on and get a fire going, maybe warm the place up. It'll be a time before I get there."

"You take care now, ya hear. It's the devil's own work what she been through."

Chapter Eight

Sydney woke in the night, the dark at first disorienting her, scaring her. She felt she was in a bed, but she didn't know where until she heard the soft snoring of another person, and her mind began to take hold. The crackle of the fire from the front room made her start, and she gasped before sinking back into the pillows and pulling covers tight around her. The pain in her jaw and around her eye was intense; opening her mouth slightly proved far too painful, and she wondered if her mandible was cracked. Her left eye was more or less squeezed shut. But what hurt most of all was that she had killed three men. Was it three? Or was it four? Vague memories ate at her; one would drift in and then fly out, leaving a feeling of wonder and dissatisfaction in its place.

And nausea.

She tried to pull the events together, make sense of them, but in her mind's eye all she saw were the flames, heard the taunts of those men, smelled the fire and the stench of their bodies, felt the weight of a man trying to rape her, and tasted fear.

She recalled the spring of the clasp knife and the sensation of it sinking into human flesh. Not surgery, as she had been trained to do, but taking the life of someone who was trying to do her harm. And the recoil of the gun, the blast in her ear as she fired sightlessly into the black night trying to stop the attack, trying to stop the whole nightmare.

She listened to Shiloh's even breathing, the in and the out of his soft snuffle, the slight whistle. In a fingernail of moonlight she could just make out his form scrunched into a chair by the bedside, his head hanging over his chest, his long legs propped up on the side of the bed, hands loose in his lap. Had he killed, too? Had he got to any of her attackers? She couldn't recall for sure how many there'd been, but she thought four. Parmeter. What had happened to Parmeter? Had he got away? Or had Shiloh caught him?

Shiloh. *All those criticisms of him, all those fine words about not killing. Where are they now? I'm no better. I have killed three men, maybe four.*

She pulled up her knees and huddled into herself, wrapped herself in the bedclothes. The scent of Shiloh was in this bedding—traces of leather and hay and straw and horse and sweat. It both comforted her with its ordinariness and distressed her, instilling a desire she knew would never be fulfilled. Never.

In the morning, she heard the sounds of breakfast preparation. Two voices. The other must be Bones. Men crashing about the kitchen, cooking. She pulled into a tight ball, unable to open the eye still. Her face ached, and she knew what she must look like. Then there were footsteps and the scrape of the chair pulled toward the bed, the clink of a spoon or other piece of cutlery against crockery, the creak of the chair as someone sat.

She felt a gentle hand on her head, fingers running through her unkempt hair until they met a knot, then letting go with care before they started once more. She sensed him bending over her, lightly resting his chin for a moment.

"Sydney?" he whispered.

In answer, she pulled the blanket higher over her head and rolled away.

"You have to eat, sweetheart. And you sure need water or something to drink. Bones made you some soup, and you don't want to insult Bones' cooking. He takes pride in it."

Her reply was to pull the blanket even tighter.

"If this is because of the swellings, I've already seen them. They'll soon go, and you'll be just as beautiful as you were before." He waited. "I may not be a doctor, but I sure as hell know you need to eat and drink. Don't make me have to sit you up. Come on now." Another moment passed. "Sydney?"

She could hear the footsteps of another man, Bones, no doubt, the uneven tread of his boot heel on the wood floor until he stopped, stood off a ways.

There was a long silence. Sydney felt they must be mouthing something to each other but wasn't sure. She began to feel the heat of the room, wrapped so tight in the blankets, and loosened them up a slight bit.

"Sydney, there's nothing here to be scared of. Bones nor I would never let anything happen to you here. I know I didn't do a great job of looking after you like I promised…" There was a hitch in Shiloh's voice, and she heard the sound of the dish being left by the bedside.

"Maybe I can feed her," Bones said.

The chair scraped away, and there were steps out of the room—Shiloh leaving, no doubt.

The chair creaked again, and there was a thump of

it getting closer. She could feel Bones' presence, a calm and a warmth. A gaunt hand folded back the blanket with care, and Bones smiled down at her.

"I know you hungry. Or at least thirsty. You want me to help you sit up?"

She gave the merest shake of her head no.

"But you gonna eat. You know you hafta. We gonna get you strong again."

She squinted at the kind face, the determination written there in gentle features that had seen their own troubles and cares. She didn't want to give him any more concerns than he'd already had, nor insult his good intentions.

She scrambled herself to a sitting position and held the blanket across her chest.

Bones took up the bowl of soup and the spoon and started to feed her, but she found she could hardly open her mouth. When most of the first spoonful ran down her cheek, and Bones was forced to dab her face with the edge of a sheet, she shook her head.

"I'll do smaller spoons, then, and sort of drizzle it in your mouth."

Outside, Shiloh paced his front porch, going through everything he had done regarding Parmeter and how he had let this happen. He blamed himself, hated himself for letting Sydney get so hurt, almost murdered like his sister. What could he have done differently? When she told him about Parmeter and that she had already informed the man of Shiloh's intentions, should he have taken her into his custody there and then? She wouldn't have agreed. Should he have gone after the man straight away? Most likely he wouldn't have been permitted into the fort, and if he had, could he have shot

Parmeter in front of everyone? That would be suicidal. He wasn't sure if he were making excuses for himself, but he didn't see what else he could have done other than what he had.

But now?

Yeager hadn't been part of this episode, but he was sure Yeager had been in on his sister's murder. So he had two men to find. Two men to kill.

The homestead door opened and Bones came out. "She asleep now. Ate some, but it was difficult. Her mouth still too swollen, and it's a load of work for her to swallow, but I got some in. We'll let her be. Sleep is good."

Shiloh shook his head in compliance. "I've got to go and report the bodies to the sheriff. Then I'm going to the fort, Bones. I won't rest easy 'til I know what happened to Parmeter. Maybe he's dead, maybe he's alive and telling lies. Either way, I've got to know. And I think Sydney will want to know, too."

"Best be saddling up, then."

"I don't want Sydney left alone, Bones. You stay here. Look after her for me. Maybe if you could get feed out to the horses and do some chores, but keep your gun by your side. 'Til this is all over, I think it best we keep watch."

****

Autumn was taking hold and the air had that mix of remnants of summer warmth and the promise of winter chill. Where trees still had leaves, they were a host of colors ranging from bright yellows to dark browns, the aspens' gold reaching into the deep blue of the sky. One day it would be nice to be able to enjoy it. One day it would be nice to be sitting out on the porch after a day's work, wife with a baby in her arms, talking over the day. Wife? Sydney.

Town seemed quiet as he trotted in, still turning over in his mind how to get to Parmeter, how to find Yeager. He tied up Whiskey in front of the sheriff's office and stood a moment to collect his thoughts before entering.

The room stank of cigarette smoke and uneaten food. The look on the sheriff's face wasn't welcoming. He lowered his legs from his desk and leaned in.

"What in tarnation is it now, Coltrane? You come to toss more insults my way, then?"

"I've come to tell you, Sheriff, Sydney Cantrell was attacked night before last—"

"Who the hell is Sydney Cantrell?"

Shiloh sighed. "Doctor Cantrell?" His hands rested at his waist, his impatience with the lawman growing by the second. He flicked a fly away from his face.

"Oh, that doctor woman who set up shop in the mercantile? So what happened?"

"Place was burnt out and she was nearly murdered. Same scene as my sister's. Parmeter and three others involved. I don't think Yeager was in on this one."

"Well, Yeager…Yeager is nowhere to be seen. Marshal come in yesterday asking about Yeager. Told him what I could, which ain't much. Nothing more than what I told you. So what happened to the doctor?" His voice was a gritty growl of disinterest.

"They burnt down her cabin, attacked her pretty bad."

"And where is she now? Does she need protection?"

"Nope. She managed to get off two shots and used

a knife on one. There're three bodies in the rubble for you to collect. Doctor's at my place, recovering."

The sheriff's brow raised.

Shiloh noted the surprise on his face but decided against explanations.

"I guess she's got nowhere else to go."

Shiloh let him have the last word on that, believing no comment was necessary and would only lead to gossip. "I'm off to find Parmeter. Doctor says Parmeter was one of the men who attacked her and she thinks she got a bullet into him."

Sheriff Barnes held his head in his hands and nodded. "Parmeter'll be back at the fort if he's still alive. I reckon you know that by now. They'll want to know what happened, come asking questions and throwing up dust. Pain in the ass."

Shiloh tapped his foot several times. "So you knew all along where Parmeter was."

"I did. But telling you was just trouble, Coltrane. You know that as well as I."

"I know you want a quiet life, Sheriff, but the only way you're going to get one is for this to be over—I find my sister's murderers and the men who attacked Doctor Cantrell. And I mean to start by trying to get into the fort to see what happened to Parmeter."

"You do that, Coltrane."

Shiloh paced a few steps. "Thing is, I'm not quite sure how."

"You're his kin, ain't you?"

"What do you mean?"

"If Parmeter was shot, I'd think they'd let you in to see him as you're probably his only kin."

He stood for a moment staring down at the sheriff,

turning this over in his mind. "Worth a try."

And he was gone.

****

Sydney awoke with a start from another nightmare to find herself alone in a comfortable bedroom, curtains gently ruffled by a breeze. She eased back into the present moment, settled against pillows, inhaled the smell of a ranch life, a gentle life attached to the land. Suddenly, the pain of the bruises didn't bother her. She felt a peace she hadn't known for a long time and decided to enjoy it before she would have to face facts.

Facts. One was she knew she was in love with Shiloh Coltrane but could never have him. A man who was a born killer, however gentle he might be, would always be looking over his shoulder at retribution, and she couldn't live like that. Second, she was engaged to Garnforth Willis and knew her life belonged back east where attacks such as what she had sustained didn't happen, to her knowledge, and civilization ruled. Yet three, she actually loved the wildness here as well as the wilderness, the unruly life with no expectations of how the next day would turn out, the mix of people, most of whom seemed to be escaping something back east or trying to make a new life for themselves. While refinements seemed to be slowly seeping in and a new century, to her belief, would bring the modernization the East now enjoyed, she knew the West would always have a certain amount of untamed society within it, a lack of the cultural progress she would enjoy in Philadelphia.

Somewhere a door slammed, and she heard whistling before Bones stuck his head around the frame.

"Ah! You awake now. Good to see that. Lookin' less peaky, too."

She smiled but wondered if her lips showed that or some horrid mimicry of a smile.

"I get you somethin' to eat, Doc. I'll be along shortly."

She nodded her thanks and nestled back into the pillows; her eyes drifted shut for a moment. In her daydream, Shiloh came loping, smiling, and he was finished with killing, done with his sister's murderers. There were golden fields, and grazing horses and cattle, and Bones rocked on the front porch while she saw patients in a back room before she went to help with dinner. Maybe there were children, too. She smiled to herself, enjoyed that moment, but then her thoughts went to Garnforth. Philadelphia society. A comfortable home, well furnished. Dinner parties with intellectual discussions, stimulating dialogs about the medical profession, the country at large, advances in medicine. She could see herself sharing an office with Garnforth, having rooms for the two of them; maybe she would specialize in women's health and obstetrics while he would choose another area in which to practice.

"You awake?"

Bones' voice was nothing more than a whisper as she heard the uneven tramp of his footsteps entering the room.

"I got you some stew now. Let's see if'n you can eat this up, huh?"

She opened her eyes and tried to smile again. There was still pain around her mouth and jaw, and she knew it would last for a week or two. Somewhere inside her, silence seemed to be in control and she couldn't speak, but she nodded at Bones as he settled into the chair beside the bed, bowl in one hand, spoon in the other.

"Small amounts, now." Bones got up a swallow on the spoon and brought it toward Sydney with care.

She managed to get it in, but it was slow chewing, her jaw and cheeks still aching. The old man had great patience, however, and sat until she waved him away.

"Gonna get you more water. You need to drink."

Sydney's voice sounded as if she were drunk, the words snatched by her swollen lips. "You're a very good nurse, Bones."

He gave her a smile like sunshine. "You a very good patient."

She took a sip from the cup he offered, but it was difficult to get much in. Sydney wiped away dribble with her sleeve, realizing for the first time she'd been put into a man's nightshirt at some stage. She felt heat rise and handed back the cup. "Where's Shiloh?" she mumbled.

"Well, I guess there's no use in lyin'. Shiloh set out to find Parmeter, but he's gone to report the bodies to the sheriff first."

At this the doctor shivered, remembered her own use of the knife and gun, her fear of the men. She slid down a bit on the bed and stared ahead.

Bones waited.

"Why...why did he become a killer, Bones? Why did he do that?"

Bones took a deep breath and put the cup he'd been holding down by the bed. "Oh, I don't know. He really a good man at heart and he hates to see injustice. All them men he killed, they deserved it."

"But why? Why didn't he just stay here and run the

ranch instead of his sister getting it all?"

"Well, he and his daddy never got on, from what I can tell. Daddy didn't think much of Shiloh. Like all young men, he had his oats to sow, and his daddy thought him worthless. So he left. My opinion, he anything but worthless. Works hard, takes the more difficult jobs on here for himself, never complains 'bout any of it, saves his money." His tone became lighter. "Gonna make a good husband one day."

Sydney kept her face ahead. *Not mine, however. Not mine.*

She changed the subject. "And how did you get the name 'Bones'?"

"Oh!" He chuckled and sat back. "Shiloh called me that, first day, said I was nothing but skin and bones, so he called me Bones. I don't mind, don't mind at all. Name I got belong to slave. That was long time ago, long before you born, even. They give us a name, we had to have it, take their last name, too. That's not my name, not a name my mama give me."

"But you were willing to take the name Shiloh gave you?"

"Shiloh saved my life, so I honor him by taking what he call me. It don't matter none. I know who I am."

Sydney's head fell back against the pillow, and she stared at the ceiling. *I wish I knew who I am now.*

****

Shiloh's horse was in a lather when he got up to the fort. The guards stared down at him from the terreplein, their rifles at the ready.

"What do you want?" one of them called down.

"Parmeter. Is he here? I heard he was hurt. I'm his

brother…" *In-law*, he mumbled under his breath.

The two guards exchanged glances and peered back down at Shiloh. There was nothing to indicate he had any ill intentions. The gate swung open.

"Hospital," one shouted down, pointing the way.

Shiloh took a deep breath, sat back, and trotted in. He got a few curious looks, but no one made any effort to further interrogate him or stop him. *Easy as pie.*

The hospital was off on its own, away from the main offices and quarters, probably to avoid the spread of any contagions. He left Whiskey ground-tied near a clump of grass that would hold his interest for a time and went inside.

The smell of carbolic hit him, mixed with sweat, medicinal potions, and other unpleasant odors.

A sergeant looked up from a desk. "Can I help you?"

"I'm looking for Oswald Parmeter. Heard he was poorly. I'm his brother-in-law."

The officer scanned him with disapproval as if he were considering whether to let him pass or not, then picked up his pen. "Second floor, first door on the right." And then, "Wait a moment."

Shiloh stopped in his tracks and swiveled around in slow motion.

"You don't know how this happened to him, do you? He said some whore shot him in town. We'll need to press charges."

Shiloh ran through a series of thoughts, uncertain. "What was he doing in town, then? With a whore?"

The sergeant puckered his mouth. "Well, I guess your sister passed on?"

"Yes."

"So…"

"The woman's run off. Sheriff said there was no case. Parmeter was forcing his attentions on her, and she wasn't liking it. I'd tell whoever to leave it be."

The sergeant sat back in his chair as if it was his decision as to how to proceed.

Shiloh nodded and took the steps two at a time.

The place was quiet, few people around, some moans coming from down the hall. He entered Parmeter's ward without knocking and glanced about. One body in a bed, curled up in white sheets. Parmeter at last.

There was a wood chair by the bedside. Shiloh grabbed it and swung it around, his arms resting on the top of the back as he stared down at his nemesis. How many months had he waited to see this man? How long had he carried hatred and the desire for retribution? He felt both cheated of the gratification of revenging his sister and pleasure the job had been done for him. Except it was Sydney who now suffered for having done it.

Or would Parmeter survive?

He rose up and tossed the chair aside.

Parmeter blinked his eyes open, tried to focus on the man who stood over him. "Who the hell are you?" he murmured. "What the hell do you want?" It must have struck him that this cowboy, this man with two guns on his hips and a look of violent loathing was not here to pay a get-well visit. Parmeter pulled his sheet up farther toward his chin and moved slightly as if he could get away.

"Don't you know who I am, Parmeter? I'm your brother-in-law, Margaret's brother, Shiloh. You remember your wife, don't you? The one you had murdered."

Parmeter gasped for air. "It was a mistake. I never meant for her or the boy…"

"It was a mistake, all right." He grabbed the pillow from under Parmeter's head and played with it, tossed it around.

Parmeter flinched and wheezed as if he couldn't take in air. "Yeager. Yancy Yeager did it," he croaked.

Shiloh held the pillow still, watching a single feather drift to the bed, lazy, taking time. "Where is Yeager now, Parmeter? Where's his hideout?"

"I don't know." It came out as a rasp, the dying man's eyes widening at the pillow, the knowledge he wouldn't be able to fight off Coltrane if he decided to smother him.

"You meet him at The Painted Lady. You're friends with him. I say you do know where he goes."

"You'll never find him. No one can find those men. They have a hideout somewhere you can't get into. Or they go down to Colorado, to the mountains." Parmeter's panic was rising, his eyes shifting from Shiloh to the pillow and back as the gunman started to toss the pillow once more, slower this time.

"Mountains. What mountains? We're in the mountains."

"Down Colorado. Across the border. One of them parks, they call them. Winter Park or Estes Park, someplace like that."

Shiloh leaned over the other man, the pillow inches from his face. "Which one, Parmeter? Which one?"

"Estes Park, then. He has a cabin in the town, lives with a woman named Claudine, French whore or something." His eyes flicked to the pillow again and back to Shiloh's face. "I didn't do it. I swear. I just meant for them to scare her so she'd sign over the ranch. Your father'd entailed it on the two of you so it wasn't mine by marriage. She kept threatening to leave me, turn me out, and that ranch, that ranch…"

Shiloh's pent-up anger came bursting through his fist. He caught Parmeter under the jaw, against the shoulder, exactly where the bullet had got him. In an instant blood was flowing from the wound once more, bright red against the white of the sheets.

Shiloh could hear the man choking as the same blood entered his lungs and he gurgled his last words. He stared down as the life went out of Parmeter, then he eased the pillow back under the dying man's head and left the room. His boot heels rang on the steps as he went down to the front desk.

"I think he needs help," he said, and went out the door.

Chapter Nine

Over the next week, Sydney made a slow recovery, the swelling going down but leaving in its wake dark blue under her eyes and lip, which would eventually turn green and yellow, she knew. And what would Garnforth make of this? Better he not know.

Shiloh was home, sleeping now in the bunkhouse as did Bones, but tending her needs as best he could, saying little. He brought her the remains of ice from his icehouse to pack on her bruises, and sat with her as she held it to her swollen face. She wondered what he planned, whom he was aiming to kill. She wasn't surprised when he stood in the doorway one afternoon, uncertainty lining his face like an unwanted guest, and strode to the bed, took the chair, and flipped it round. He said nothing as he sat and rested his chin on his crossed hands and gazed at her.

Once more, she felt like meat on his dish.

"You'll be up soon, I reckon."

"I could be up now, but the two of you are like mother hens. Plus, of course, I haven't any clothes."

"Bones went in and got you a ready-made dress. He wasn't sure if it would fit but reckoned it to be about your size."

"And underclothes?"

Shiloh took a breath and suppressed a smile. "Well, he wasn't going in for that. I'm afraid... I guess your nightdress will have to do for now."

"*Your nightshirt* won't do, Shiloh. If I give him a list?"

"I'll go. It'll raise some eyebrows, but I reckon enough people know by now—"

"What do they know?"

Shiloh hesitated. "That you're here. That you were attacked and I took you in."

"For which, thanks."

Shiloh's head tilted. "I haven't made it a secret I'm in love with you, Syd."

She had to smile, as skewed as it might be. No one had ever called her "Syd" and yet it pleased her.

"Listen, I…I kept this from you 'cause I wasn't sure how you'd take it: Parmeter's dead. He died of his wound. Your shot got him in the shoulder and while, apparently, he might have survived, he…he died of infection." Shiloh bit his lip, and his gaze met hers.

"I don't think that's quite the truth. Other than, of course, I shot him."

He took in a large gulp of air and sat back. "I visited him. I wanted to know…there's another man, a man named Yeager, I have to find before I'm finished with all this. He was the one who killed Meg—my sister—and I…all I've been doing these past months is procrastinating, leaving it be—"

"Maybe that was wise?"

"I don't think so. I came back here because I was tired of killing, tired of being a hired gun. Then I walked right into my sister's death, my nephew's death, and I was back where I had always been. So I left it. Made excuses. I didn't know where Parmeter was. I didn't know where Yeager was. Yet all the time they'd been right under my nose, meeting in The Painted Lady, Parmeter at the fort. I was sick of the killing, Syd. I couldn't face the fact I had to do more, but I knew I had to. Then you come along. If I had dealt with Parmeter right when I got back, this wouldn't have happened to you. It'll eat me to my dying day."

"Don't be ridiculous. It wasn't your responsibility to go after Parmeter!"

"'Course it was. Who else should avenge Meg's death? But I kept putting it off, making excuses, because—"

"Well, they say revenge is a dish best eaten cold."

"What the heck does that mean?"

"It means…it means it's best to wait to take your revenge because it'll be more satisfying. The foe won't be expecting it by then."

Shiloh blinked a few times, lifted his head for another deep breath, and leaned forward, rested his chin on the chair back for a second. "Well. Maybe that's true. I've never thought about it, to be honest. But what I know now is I have one more man to get and—"

"Why? Why do you think it's your job to get this man, this killer? Why isn't it the sheriff's job, or the U.S. marshal's?"

"Because I've given them months to do it and they haven't lifted a finger, that's why. And because I won't rest easy 'til it's done. I want to get on with my life, don't you know that? I want to live here, see to the ranch, marry, have children. I'm done with all the killing—"

Sydney raised her voice. "If you're done with the killing, then leave it! Leave it, Shiloh! Let it be! Because there's never a last one, is there? There'll always be another reason to kill, another gunman around the corner wanting to take you on, another person who needs a hired gun."

"And I'll say 'no.' " His voice was quiet, steady.

Her voice modulated as well. "I don't think you can, Shiloh. I don't think you're capable of saying 'no.' "

****

In the evening he leant against the porch rail, the setting sun casting a green glow along the ridge above the ranch, the cattle content and grazing before they settled for the night. It was a scene he knew well, remembered from his childhood, the family outside doing their final chores, his mama watching from the porch, wiping her hands on her apron and enjoying the moment. Why had he left it all? Not more than seventeen years old and he had left it all behind after one final argument with his father, Meg standing in the background shouting to stop it, stop it. If he had, would she be here today?

Shorter days were pulling in the light and the chill air spoke of winter to come. It brushed against his skin like a rejected lover trying to win him back—unwanted, uninvited. There'd be no use now of trying to find Yeager 'til the spring; that would be a fool's errand, for the mountain passes would be saddle-deep with snow soon, and finding Yeager would be impossible, wherever he was. Or was he once again making excuses? The thought crossed his mind that if he gave up, perhaps Sydney would stay. She had nowhere else to go, apparently, unless the reservation gave her a place or she stayed in the small office she had there. He realized then he didn't know her plans, they hadn't discussed it, and maybe it was better that way, for if he started to ask she might take it on herself to up and leave.

In the morning, he headed into town to buy her undergarments and get the mail, watching out, always watching now, to see if Yeager were there.

Dismounting in front of the post office, tying Whiskey, he heard the familiar gruff voice of the sheriff nearby and hoped to avoid him.

"Wait up, Coltrane!"

No use. He turned to meet the sheriff's gaze, then pivoted on his heel, let the man follow him to the grille.

"Coltrane mail, please, and Cantrell. Anything for Dr. Cantrell?"

"She with you still?" The sheriff's annoyance was evident.

"Yup."

The postmaster handed the letters through the slot, and Shiloh stepped aside.

"I need to talk with her. About what happened."

"Why?"

"Parmeter's dead, and the other three. Seems quite a feat for a little lady."

"You think I was there? If I'd been there, Sheriff, she wouldn't be lying over at my ranch busted up the way she is. And her cabin wouldn't be burnt down. No way they would have even gotten near her."

"So you say. But I haven't seen exactly how 'busted up' she is."

"You've seen the cabin, though."

"Coltrane, people do things for a lot of strange reasons."

Shiloh gawped at him and took a step back. "You

saying she burnt down her own cabin?"

"Now, take it easy, son. I'm not saying anything of the kind. But I think it's my job to hear what happened."

"And you have. You heard it from me."

"And you're no relation."

"And you're not questioning her and upsetting her any more than she has been." He started off for the mercantile, turned suddenly, nose to nose with the sheriff. "And by the way, I'm just off to buy her...her undergarments since everything she had was lost!"

But when he came out of the mercantile, Sheriff Barnes was standing there, the reins to both his horse and Whiskey in his hand.

****

Bones and Shiloh both seemed to have a good eye for her size. The dress was a margin too big, but Bones had said he planned it that way as she surely would gain back some weight after her ordeal. Shiloh, surprisingly, had been spot on in his choices.

She straightened her hair with a brush of his left by the washbasin, long strands of blonde hair snagged in the bristles. There was no point in trying to clean it for him or for her use, so she just tugged the brush through her hair and then braided it.

Outside, the three men all stood waiting, barely glancing at each other. They sprang to life as she stepped outside. Bones gave a low whistle, but it was the sheriff who spoke first.

"I'm sorry to put you through this, Dr. Cantrell."

"So you should be," retorted Shiloh.

Sydney gave him a sideways glance and murmured, "It's fine."

"I better get some tea and coffee." Bones headed for the door.

"Make it whiskey for me." Shiloh was obviously set on showing his disapproval. "You best sit down, Syd. How do you feel?"

She settled herself on a bench facing the sheriff. "Fine."

"Doctor, can you tell me what happened?"

"As much as I remember. I heard horses gallop up to the cabin in the night, so I arose and grabbed both my gun and my knife—"

"You always sleep with them nearby?"

"The cabin is in a fairly isolated location, Sheriff. I'm a woman living alone. I take precautions. Or took them."

"Go on."

"Almost immediately a lit torch came flying through the window and the cabin took light. I tried to get out the back but the door was blocked, so I was forced to knock out the window. Then I was grabbed by one man who held me while another attempted to…to violate me. I got hold of my clasp knife and let it go into him."

"You stabbed him."

"I think that's self-defense? I aimed under the heart meaning to stop him, not to kill him, but with so much going on… As I staggered to my feet I saw another man and fired blindly at him…no, maybe I was grabbed first and beaten. Really, I cannot remember the train of events. I used the gun with intent to harm, not kill, but I don't believe it makes any difference in self-defense. Does it?"

Shiloh stepped forward. "I think that's enough,

Sheriff. You got the details you came for, haven't you?"

"Not quite. Dr. Cantrell, do you know of any reason why these men would have chosen to attack you in such a vicious manner?"

"I have no idea, Sheriff, what their intent was. Rape? They were animals. I was a woman on my own, an easy target." She swallowed her lie with a sideways glance at Shiloh.

"And did you recognize any of them?"

"Parmeter. I recognized Parmeter's voice."

Bones appeared with a tray of tea, coffee, and whiskey. He poured the tea for Sydney and handed it to her, but the cup rattled so badly in its saucer as she held it that she had to put it down. He left the coffee and whiskeys on the tray and went back inside.

"And how did you recognize Parmeter?" Sheriff Barnes appeared perplexed, his hands on his hips.

"I knew him to be the company clerk at the fort. I've been to speak with Colonel Wright…" She stopped and her gaze met Shiloh's, the realization of where this could lead hit her. If the sheriff bothered to ask the colonel about her visits, it might lead to Shiloh after her last visit when she accused Parmeter and told him Shiloh was after him. "Items meant for the Indian reservation go missing when his men are meant to be delivering them. I've been in to complain. And… and…"

"And?"

She peered up at the sheriff. "That's it, really. Parmeter always seemed to ogle me, make insinuating statements. Since Mr. Coltrane had reason to believe he might have been involved with the murder of his own wife, Mr. Coltrane's sister, I was very wary of him. Very."

The sheriff leaned forward and took up one of the whiskeys on the tray.

Shiloh hung back against the railing, still studying Sydney, until the sheriff turned to him.

"Well, Coltrane. Convenient—Parmeter's dead from his wounds now. Guess you'll be going after Yeager." And he slugged back the glassful.

****

She stood at the rail next to Shiloh, the warmth from his body stopping the chill she felt. Such a beautiful place, so much to live for here. When the sheriff had ridden off, a small dot in the distance, she peered over at Shiloh.

"He'll find out I warned Parmeter, and figure it out."

"I doubt that now. It makes no matter anyway. What's done is done. I think when he said I'd be going after Yeager he was hoping I'd do his job for him—he knows this has to be finished."

"And will you?"

"In the spring. I'll set out when the worst of the snow is over. There's no knowing how far I'd get now."

There was some relief to this, as if she could protect him from himself a little longer.

"You can stay here as long as you need, you know that."

"I've turned you out of your home, it seems. That's not right."

"It's right by me." Another of his lopsided smiles. "Oh. I forgot." He started for the door. "You have mail."

115

"Mail? Oh."

Shiloh disappeared for a moment, came back flapping two letters against his palm. "I was thinking…thinking I'd like to build you an office and living space in town. It'd be far safer for you in town. You could stay here 'til—"

"Shiloh. That's very kind, but I couldn't ask that of you and have no means of repaying you. And I really still owe you for the steers."

"I'm not asking for repayment. Did I say anything about payment? Or cost?" He proffered the two letters.

She glanced down at them, her brow creased.

"Pretty fancy writing on that one." He pointed. "That your professor?"

"Yes." She made no move to open it; the other took her interest. "Anyway, I can't let you do that."

"Can't let me?" He smiled. "That's a dare. You gonna stop me?"

She shrugged. "You'd be wasting your time."

"Where else you gonna work?"

"I haven't figured it out yet." Her impatience grew with the stubbornness of the man. "I thought I'd go back to the reservation, first of all."

"'Fraid you might say that. Don't like that idea."

She stomped. "And who are you to like or dislike what I do?"

That smile again. "Come on, Syd. You know you're not welcome there."

"I am welcome. To be doctor. As long as I don't cause a fuss again with the Army or the Agent."

Shiloh grunted and reached across for the whiskey still sitting on the tray. Inside, Bones was busy in the kitchen, clanging pots and pans.

Sydney flicked away an insect, then ran her fingernail under the strange letter, not really wanting to read the professor's in front of Shiloh. Her mouth dropped open as she unfolded it, read it, and passed it to him.

Dr. Cantrell,

I regret to inform you that the Dept. of the Interior has now suspended your temporary contract in favor of a full-time male physician. We will therefore no longer be requiring your services.

Yours faithfully,

Manfred Morris,

Indian Agent

"Well, that settles it, then. New office and new living place in town."

She ignored him and stepped to the bench, plunked herself down. She decided to open the letter from Garnforth and read slowly, feeling Shiloh's gaze upon her.

Sept. 29 1899

Dearest Sydney,

Let me first say I can understand the pull of this adventure to a young woman of your spirit—any woman who has taken on the years of study to become a physician and withstood the tests such labor puts upon her must have a strength of character and fortitude that would welcome such a life. But remember, my dear, we are not forever young, nor will your talents be appreciated in such a society as you describe.

Sydney, my admiration and fondness for you is genuine, and I offer you a comfortable home with a bright future, a future that represents all for which you have worked. Do not let this slip away from us, my dear, for the uncertainty of this wilderness life you have lived.

Return to me soon, my darling. Let us marry and face our future together.

Yours fondly,
Garnforth

She folded the letter and slipped it into her pocket. She didn't say anything to Shiloh but met his gaze, his curiosity all too obvious on his face.

"It wasn't bad news, was it?" he tried.

"No. Not bad news."

He shifted his stance and took a deep breath. "Well. I'm gonna build that office for you, and the living quarters with a kitchen and all. Make it nice. Homey and welcoming."

She stared at him. Held herself against the desire to run and kiss him and keep him to herself.

"You stay here 'til then. You can put word out to your town patients if they need you, this is where to find—"

"Shiloh…"

He stopped. "But I really think we should be married. So people don't talk. You know. I should probably get down on one—"

"Shiloh."

"One knee…"

He glanced across at her, the yearning in his eyes breaking her heart, pain in her being, her own longing making her ill.

"Marry me. Marry me, Sydney."

"I'm sorry, Shiloh. I can't. I'm going to be married to someone else."

Part Two — Chapter Ten

Gray. All gray.

The train slowed as it came into the city, passed buildings several stories high, brick and cement and stone instead of trees and mountains, lines of houses instead of the rolling plains. Shiloh's last words to her still rang in her head: "I'll be waiting for you. I'll be doing the house and office in town like I promised." She had shaken her head, "No," but he'd just given her a slow, knowing smile, bent and kissed her hand above the glove, and helped her onto the train.

She still felt his lips on her wrist.

As the train now halted beside the platform, she shuffled into the coat Shiloh had bought her, a lambs' wool he had seen in town, dark blue he said would remind her of the Wyoming sky. She fetched her bag, again filled with a few items she had let him purchase to see her through the journey. All reminders of him. As if she needed that.

Her carriage was at the very end of the platform, and she had the length of it to walk, spotting Garnforth in his dapper velvet-collared coat and new-style trilby hat. He waited for her to come to him. No running into each other's arms like some young lovers might do.

He held her at arm's length to look her over, then took her bag and looped her arm through his as he led her toward the station exit.

"Good journey?"

"Long." She found it difficult to look at him and smile, but she forced herself to do so.

"You seem tired."

"Yes."

"I…I have to say there'll be talk about you living with me, but I've asked Mrs. Henshaw, the housekeeper, to stay over. As chaperone. Until we are married. I thought as soon as possible, my dear. So there is no more talk than need be. I don't want to put my position at the university in jeopardy. You understand that."

"Yes." She pondered this news. "I think…I think, however, I need some time. To adjust back to Philadelphia. Rest."

"Oh, my goodness, you'll be back in the rounds of Philadelphia in no time. And I'm sure you will have plenty of time to rest." He looked her over. "You're looking very country, I must say. Have you no other gowns?"

"No. Nothing." She thought for a moment and decided against telling him the whole gruesome story right away. "I wore mostly a divided skirt, indispensable for riding there. I left that as not decent for Philadelphia."

"Very wise. But you appear somewhat… somewhat…how shall I say without hurting your feelings? The braid and all. Very rural."

She stopped and unlooped her arm, peered up at his kind face, the lack of comprehension written there. "It's a very different life, Garnforth. It will take me time to readjust. I hope you understand."

There was some hesitancy when he said, "Yes.

Yes, of course."

She remained silent in the carriage, not listening to his stream of gossip, university news, what he had read in medical newspapers, mutual acquaintances' rumors. The streets went by, a never-ending gyroscope of neat buildings, trim brick or stone houses, orderly roads with the occasional newfangled horseless carriage making its way with a squawk of its horn. Sporadically there were children playing hoops or balls or skipping ropes.

She hated it.

Too much motion, too much of man's progress that was not for the good. Not enough nature or beauty or silence. Too many people. *Things.*

And yet she had been brought up here, gone to school and university here, never knowing there was something else, something better.

Would she ever get used to it again?

"I think it best you contact your parents, Sydney." His words suddenly woke her to his conversation. He took her hand.

"No."

"I think it best. I really must insist you make amends with your father. He is a powerful man in the city now."

"No." She met his gaze with the stubborn set of her uplifted chin and her unyielding eyes.

"All right," he conceded. "We'll discuss this later. When you perhaps feel better rested and have had time to consider."

"I won't be changing my mind." She glanced out the carriage to avoid his disapproval.

"We'll see. I think when you've rested and heard…well, when we've discussed it further, you'll understand the importance of it."

But in her mind and heart she was already headed back to Wyoming. Already breathing fresh air.

Already in Shiloh's arms.

****

Shiloh stood at the sawmill trying to figure out how much timber he would need initially to frame the house. He had selected a vacant spot, almost in the center of town, and knew Sydney would appreciate that location. He'd never built a two-story structure before but figured there couldn't be too much difference to what he'd previously done. Standing there with his pencil and a piece of paper, he was trying to figure the amount of timber needed, but his math wasn't good, and his head swam with the numbers.

Joe, the merchant, studied him with impatience and tapped a foot. "You doing balloon framing, right?"

"Yup."

"All right, then. I'll figure it. How many floors?"

"Two." Shiloh showed him his sketch with the measurements, and Joe figured it up for him.

"Looks inner-resting. What's it gonna be?"

"Doctor's office with a living area upstairs."

"Doctor's office? For what doctor?"

"Doctor Cantrell, of course. She's been using the back room of the mercantile. No good. She needs a real good office if we want her to stay." Shiloh suppressed a smile.

"Shiloh, she's already gone. Went back east. Didn't you hear?"

"Nope, she's coming back. Only gone to visit her family and rest up a bit after what happened. She'll come back. And when she does, she'll find a bright new shiny office waiting for her."

"Well. She must be going to rest for a dang long time, 'cause with winter settin' in and all, I doubt you'll get this done any time soon."

"We'll see."

****

"I know Doctor Iona was fond of you, and probably would approve of this arrangement, but I have to tell you, I do not. I served that dear lady for fifteen years; I was distraught at her passing, and I fail to see how Dr. Garnforth can make this decision so soon after his wife's death. Nor marry someone so much his junior." Mrs. Henshaw didn't mince her words. She stood before an exhausted Sydney, her hands folded in front of her apron, her back ramrod straight, her hair combed back in a tight bun. "However, I will serve you to the best of my ability, as Dr. Garnforth wishes, while you are a guest in this house."

I'm supposed to be more than a guest.

Sydney felt like a child who had been smacked by her nanny, but kept her thoughts to herself. "Thank you," was all she said before she stood and went to the bag left on a chair.

"I think you're aware the Willises always dress for dinner." Mrs. Henshaw peered straight ahead at her, then marched to the door and left her alone.

The room seemed sumptuous after her Wyoming cabin—velvet drapes, heavily upholstered chairs, a carved mahogany bed that would suit a king, and a dressing table with an ornate mirror. She took a peek in this mirror, noting a small area of faded yellow under her jaw where she had been hit. Garnforth hadn't noticed, so perhaps she should proceed without telling him. She certainly didn't look her best, was no longer the bright-eyed girl who had fallen in love with the eminent, but married, professor of medicine—a man she had once worshipped and who had taken her under his wing. Well, she had made her bed and now must lie in it. There was no going back to Shiloh, no return to Wyoming. Shiloh would be off looking for the last man, hoping to kill him, and she couldn't face any more killing, couldn't face *him*, knowing his intentions.

She was wearing the plain gray dress Bones had bought, but Shiloh had purchased another before her journey, and she opened the bag to put that on. Blue like the coat, it brought out her eyes, he'd said. She couldn't stand the thought he had spent his money on her and she had left him; he still sincerely believed she would return. She'd never be able to pay him back.

She ran a comb through her hair and pinned it up, washed and changed, stepped out of the room with her nerves jangling.

In the drawing room, Garnforth stood waiting, an air of impatience hanging on him like a cloak.

"My dear, I so looked forward to seeing you dressed for the evening." His criticism was evident in his tone.

Drained of the energy to think of an acceptable excuse, she explained, "There was a fire. My cabin. I lost everything and a kind…friend…bought me this. I haven't but the two dresses, I'm afraid."

"Well, I hope this was your friend's taste rather than yours. You must go out tomorrow and purchase whatever you need. I have accounts. Pretend to be Iona; I believe they are still in her name in the women's shops."

She smiled in response, trying to concentrate on his generosity rather than the fact of Iona's accounts and his lack of care or comment regarding the fire.

Mrs Henshaw stood at the door to the dining room, her way of announcing dinner, Sydney supposed. She passed the woman in front of Garnforth, sensing the housekeeper's whiff of disapproval.

The table was set for her and Garnforth at opposite ends, four places either side between them. She knew her parents lived in a similar fashion, but when she had visited here previously there had always been other guests filling those seats. Now the distance between them seemed ridiculous and more representative of their differences than of a close, loving relationship.

He pulled out her chair and proceeded to his position, shook out his napkin as if demonstrating what to do.

Mrs Henshaw came with a silver soup tureen and ladled a portion into Sydney's soup plate, spilling some on her dress.

"Oh, I am sorry, miss."

As Sydney looked up at her, Henshaw widened her eyes almost daring the young woman to complain. Sydney only took a corner of her napkin and dabbed it into her water goblet, knowing full well such vulgarity would enrage both Garnforth and the housekeeper.

"That's quite all right, Mrs. Henshaw. As a *doctor* I'm well aware we all may develop shakes with age."

Henshaw gasped but walked on to serve Garnforth and left.

"I don't think that was necessary, my dear. Don't you think it impolite to remind one of their ineptitude, especially when caused perhaps by age?"

Sydney took a spoonful to her mouth and swallowed. She didn't look at Garnforth but proceeded to eat. "I believe she did it on purpose, Garnforth. She has made it quite clear, in fact told me, she does not approve of our relationship."

He stared at her in doubt. "I find that hard to believe, my dear."

She met his gaze. "I'm sorry. Are you calling me a liar?"

"A liar! Heavens, no! Only—"

"I'm telling you she told me, plain as day, she disapproves of our relationship, that she was devoted to Iona and—"

"And so she was. Surely she just meant she finds it difficult for Iona to be replaced."

"That is not what she said. She said—"

"I think that's enough, my dear. We'll let it pass for now."

A feeling like suffocation began to grow within her. Airless, breathless, confining. She felt smothered. It was as if something were entering her mind and stifling it. She laid her spoon down and sat quietly, unable to eat. Was it a delayed reaction to the attempted rape and murder at the cabin, the fire, the attack, the killings? Or was it being here in a city after the months in the wilderness, the comparative freedom she had enjoyed, the usefulness?

The professor glanced up. "You must be terribly tired. I'm sorry, I seem to have asked far too much of you straight away, not given you time to settle in. It is completely my fault."

She let his words comfort her. Here was more the man she had fallen in love with, considerate and kind, always looking out for her welfare.

Mrs. Henshaw came back to remove the soup, not showing any further dismay nor trying any more upsets. The silence was heavy and startling. Sydney recalled intense and lengthy conversations she had had at this table, between Garnforth and herself. New medical theories, the work of European physicians, inventions that might aid the profession, and the rights of women to become doctors. She had missed that and wondered now if it would come again, whether their interest in each other was genuine or superficial. He had fed her mind, but perhaps something was missing.

Love, she realized, had no reason, no whys or wherefores, no innate intelligence to decide whom to love, who was good for you, a sensible choice. And why be sensible? Why not throw caution to the winds and live boldly?

Yet she still asked herself if, as a doctor, a healer, she could really ever love a man who had killed for a living and would kill again.

****

Bones placed the dish of steak and beans in front of Shiloh, who almost seemed not to notice it was there.

"You been mooning over that gal since she left. I don't even know what's got inta you since you met."

"Nothing. Nothing's got into me. Sydney's got into me, that's what."

"Well, I see that. You buildin' her that Tash Mehall like that king done built to show his love for his wife."

"Huh?" Shiloh looked up, a lack of understanding wrinkling between his eyes.

"I read about that. This Indian king built a great

127

palace, all white, to show his wife how much he loved her. That what you doin'. Only in your case she ain't never gonna see it."

"What Indian? What tribe? Where is it?"

"No, no. Indian like the country. India. Shiloh, you don't read 'nuf."

Shiloh grunted. "Maybe not, but I know how to build. And I know Sydney's coming back."

"How you know that?"

"I just do. She's not meant for the city, she's meant to be out here. Helping people who really need her, not overstuffed easterners."

"So, sayin' she comes on back, what makes you think she loves you?"

He sat back and noticed his plate of food for the first time. He took up his fork and knife and started to cut into it, his half-smile creeping out against his will. "I just do, Bones. I just do know she loves me. Because when you love someone as much as I love her, it has to be returned. It just has to be."

Chapter Eleven

"I want you to deputize me."

Sheriff Barnes sat back and rocked in his chair a moment, taking in the steel gray eyes, the lines around the young man's mouth, the scar. Shiloh knew he was being studied, considered, pondered like a map to a buried treasure. He also knew the older man didn't think much of him, had an idea he was next to evil, not far different from the murderers he went after. But he also knew the sheriff needed him to do his job. Barnes would never go after Yancy Yeager; he was too old to take him on, and unless he got Yeager, more killings would happen even without Parmeter on the scene now.

The chair smacked on the floor, Barnes' boot heels clacked as he leant forward, his hands clasped on his desk in front. "Why now? After all the killings you've done, why now?"

"Those killings were legal, Sheriff. You know that. I may have been a hired gun, but I was protecting property, people, or it was in self-defense. You don't have any wanted posters on me, do you?"

"No." He swiveled toward the wall where the posters hung, then swung back to Shiloh. "There's two feet of snow out there and more to come. You think you have a hope in hell of finding Yeager now?"

"Maybe. Maybe not. But I want to be ready to go when I feel the time is right. Tracking is easier in the snow."

"If you can ride." Barnes sat back and considered. "I want to know something, Coltrane. You're a young man. Your pappy ran a good ranch, and you got that now. Seem to be doing all right, too. So what makes you feel you have to go after Yeager?"

Shiloh ran his hand across his mouth and bit his bottom lip. "I want it to be over. He killed my sister, was partially responsible for nearly killing Doctor Cantrell. I want him gone. Dead. And it appears you're not going to be doing it."

"What gives you that idea? I'm biding my time. You have information as to his whereabouts? A trail to track?"

"Seems you've been waiting a long time, Sheriff. I got an idea where he might be hiding. It's a start."

"You want to share that information with me?"

"Colorado. I got it out of Parmeter. Estes Park."

The room suddenly felt like an ice storm had blown in. Shiloh realized his mistake.

"You got it out of Parmeter?"

A clock on the wall seemed to suddenly get a lot louder.

The sheriff bit his thumb as if he were considering something, then seemed to let it go.

Shiloh kept very still and waited.

The moment passed.

Barnes rocked once again in his chair, never taking his gaze off Shiloh. "Seen you building that house up the street. What's that gonna be, then?"

"Doctor's office." He cracked his knuckles. He hadn't heard a word from Sydney, and it pained him to think she had just left and might not be coming back.

And she hadn't left him an address either, said it would be best if they didn't write, but she would try to wire him the money she owed for the clothes he had bought her. Damn, he didn't want the money. He wanted her.

"Doctor's office," the sheriff echoed, stared at his hands as if there might be something written there.

Shiloh could see a lamp come on, and he didn't think he was going to like the thought that accompanied it.

"What if you go and the doc comes back and the office is not finished for her?"

"She'll go to Bones." The certainty of his own statement surprised him, but he knew that was what she would do. He met Barnes' gaze head on, like a standoff.

Barnes tapped his foot several times, sat back again, and rocked on the chair's back legs, then came forward with a bang.

"No. Not yet."

"Not yet?"

"I'll deputize you when the time is right. Maybe. I'll think on it. Now is not the right time, Coltrane. You won't make it down to Colorado, never mind into the Rockies to Estes Park. That's a hare-brained scheme of yours, and—"

"And that's what he'll think—no one in their right mind would come after him this time of year. That's what makes it perfect, Sheriff—he won't be expecting me."

"It would take you the better part of maybe six weeks to get down there in this weather. Horse'll break a leg or you'll fall down a ravine. Listen to me. I know what I'm talking about. I'll think about deputizing you in the spring when the weather's lifting. 'Til then, you stay put, and I'll see whether I can get the marshal to do something, save you the trouble. He won't be going anywhere either—Yeager."

"I don't want to be—"

"That's final, Coltrane. You get on back to building your whatever-it-is and let me deal with this in my own way."

"Maybe I'm going to deal with it in *my* own way."

****

"Your father is a very important man in Philadelphia now, well-to-do, influential and far-reaching. It isn't wise, my dear, for you to carry on this rift and separation from your parents. Surely you can find it in your heart to go to them and try to make amends?"

"What difference does it make how influential he may be—if people, women, need a doctor, they will come to me. Garnforth, my parents do not believe a woman should have a career. How can I make amends? I would have to repudiate the fact of my education, an education you yourself, as well as Iona, helped me obtain. I would have to discontinue any medical practice, a profession for which I worked long and hard. I would be denying myself, who I am. Is that what you want?"

"I… Of course not. But perhaps you might try to explain yourself, explain how important this is to you, why you have done it."

"I did try. They don't listen. They wanted me to marry, have children, be like them."

"Do you not expect to have children?"

"Yes. Yes, of course I want to have children. One day. But I don't see why a woman can't be both a mother and a doctor."

"Who will look after the children?"

"It is possible to do both, Garnforth. With the help of a husband, or a nursery maid and a governess. Women of my background have those for their children anyway, so what difference does it make if I spend my time practicing medicine and return to my children fulfilled and happy, or spend my time in useless pursuits, playing cards and shopping?" This wasn't the man she had fallen in love with. All too evident now, he didn't see her in the same light in which he had seen Iona. She felt ill.

Garnforth paced the length of the Turkish carpet in the drawing room. Hesitantly, he said, "I think you must try, my dear. You see…you see I have a dream, too. A clinic. For the two of us, of course. I would be a chief medical officer, or administrator if you like, and you would be attending physician. Think of it, Sydney. No one to tell you what to do. You would be your own person, see patients as you wish. Wouldn't that be wonderful?"

She felt the pressure of his words. Certainly there was sense to them, and she could see herself without anyone to tell her how to perform or what to do. Would Garnforth leave her to her own decisions, her own diagnoses? But hadn't she had that in Wyoming? Then again, she had made her choice and come back to Philadelphia.

"But we need money," Garnforth continued. "Such a facility does not come cheaply. If you were to…to make amends with your parents, we would have some hope of your father perhaps providing a goodly sum toward such a clinic."

"He would stipulate I wasn't to work. I'm sure of it."

"Perhaps. But of course, once the clinic was built… In any case, I am hoping for children. Surely you would want to take time off while they are young. Then you could return to work when they are suckled."

Sydney pivoted on her heel, anger flaring. "And just how many children were you expecting to have, Garnforth? You know as well as I that as soon as one is suckled, along comes another. Were you planning on keeping me at home? Was that your intention all along?"

"Oh, no, my dear. Of course not. There are… ways…to prevent such a thing from happening."

"As a doctor, may I remind you I know of those 'ways.' "

Garnforth coughed. "Of course, of course."

For a moment, Sydney thought he would let the matter drop, but no.

"Well, we'll leave it for a week or so, let you settle in as you have expressed a wish to do so, and then I shall arrange a meeting. Lunch perhaps, or dinner."

"But I said…I don't think—"

"That is my final decision, Sydney. You will meet with your parents and you will try to make amends, or explain yourself to their satisfaction. I do not wish to force this on you, but if I must, I must. After a suitable amount of time, you will then approach your father with the idea of the clinic. For me. This is something you are well capable of doing, and something from which you will benefit as much as I."

"But I—"

"That is my final word on the matter."

And he left the room.

She stood in the new electric light, the plush carpet soft under her feet, the aroma of furniture polish in the air. Almost as if on cat's paws, it came to her that this is what he had seen in her all along, this is what he had planned, that perhaps he didn't truly love her at all but tolerated her, found her an acceptable mate, a satisfactory replacement for Iona whom he had truly loved, and a wife young enough to bear the children Iona never had. And Sydney came with the great benefit of her father's wealth. Was that it?

****

Bones came in and stomped his boots free of snow before catching them in the jack and yanking them off. "Comin' down heavy now, but the feed is out. We'll go again in the morning."

"Thanks." Shiloh continued to add up his figures on the accounts, a job he truly hated, and tried to keep his mind off Yeager, Sydney, his sister, and anyone or anything else who disturbed him. He felt Bones' presence, standing there eyeing him, and he knew Bones' hands were on his hips and he was shaking his head, most likely. He just felt it, the displeasure of the other man, the irritation.

"You still workin' those accounts?"

"Uh-mmm." He didn't look up. He dotted the end of a line and broke the point of his pencil, blowing out his anger as he sat back.

"And now what?"

"Now I've broken the point." He pulled up his knife from the top of his boot and started to pare the pencil.

"Well, I'll be gettin' dinner together. And when

that's done you better be in a better mood than what I sees now, or I'll just toss the dang steak out and let you fetch it up yourself." He moved toward the range and the icebox.

"Hmm." Shiloh noted the curls of pencil wood as they landed on the table, like curls of hair, and shaved the pencil to a fine point. "This still doesn't add up."

"Your figures?"

"What else?'

"I don't know. Maybe you was thinkin' of that woman again."

"I never stop thinking of her. I just get on with other things."

Bones came back toward the table. He kept his gaze on Shiloh as the younger man doodled some in the corner of the sheet where he'd been writing. "Well, now. I wish I had some great words of advice for you, or some way to help you out. But there ain't none. What's gonna happen is gonna happen, she either come on back here or she don't, and I don't see nothing you can do either way 'ceptin' to take what gonna happen. So you best be addin' up your sums, doin' your accounts and all, and wait to see what unrolls here, 'cause that's all you can do, and not a thing more."

Shiloh tapped the pencil three times, then dropped it from a height and watched as it rolled over the edge of the table and fell. He made no move to pick it up, but didn't expect Bones to either. Yet Bones, after a moment, bent and clasped it and placed it with care on the table so it wouldn't roll off once more.

"There're jobs need to be done here. You the boss, but I'm not doin' every dang thing roundabouts here. You hear me?"

"It's Yeager. He's sitting pretty as you please in his hideout, knowing I want to come after him but can't 'cause he's down in Colorado and I'm a long ride away in good weather. In this, well…"

" 'Well' is right. You can't do what you can't do, and you can't control what you can't control, and that's an end to it."

And with that, the old man went back to fixing dinner.

****

"Garnforth," she began, and set her spoon by the side of her plate. "You know…I have no money of my own now, having returned from Wyoming as promised, and having lost all my possessions in the fire."

He peered at her across the length of table, his spoon halfway to his mouth. Saying nothing, he swallowed the spoonful and set the spoon down by the side of his soup plate. "You are going to ask me for money?"

"Yes. I'm afraid so."

"It would be best to ask your father, don't you think?"

Sydney's mouth opened, and she clamped it shut again. "You know…you know I cannot do that."

"And I cannot lend you money unless you agree to speak with your father on the matter I have already discussed." He resumed spooning up his soup, ignored her silence and stare.

"I see." She served herself a mouthful, head tilted in thought. "I was under the impression I was to receive an allowance. Housekeeping."

"Mrs. Henshaw is in charge of housekeeping. You have access to a number of accounts for your fripperies and clothes."

"I've never asked for that. But I am asking for a small sum with which to repay the friend who lent me money for new clothes and train fare with which to return here."

"I will send it myself then. How much do you owe?"

Sydney maintained her composure, trying to figure a way in which to return the money to Shiloh without Garnforth knowing it was a man. *Shiloh*? Would that do the trick? "I believe forty dollars would be sufficient."

Garnforth peered at her, no doubt assessing whether she was telling the truth. "If you write out her name and address, I will make sure it is sent. In return—"

"I can save you the trouble and send it myself. It is but a small sum. Do you not trust me with it?"

His gaze sized her up keenly. "Yes. Of course I do, but—"

"In return I shall attempt to speak with my father."

"That's my girl."

Chapter Twelve

Shiloh ran the plane a couple more times to make sure the door fit perfectly, opened and closed it, listened that the catch was hitch-free. He ran his hand down the satin feel of the wood, pleased with his accomplishment, the perfect proportions of the house and office, the thought that went into the various rooms even though he knew little of a doctor's requirements. The upstairs quarters, he felt, would suit any couple, never mind a single woman—which he hoped Sydney wouldn't be for long. He had spent hours on this structure and, heaven forbid, if she never returned, it would sell well and be useful for someone else.

But she had to return. He had never known a woman like Sydney, educated, concerned with people, always wanting to help and do for others. And beautiful to boot.

"How's Coltrane's Folly going?" Joe, the timber merchant, called up from the boardwalk. "Looks pretty good. Guess my figures were right, then."

"Yup. Thanks for that, Joe." He snapped out of his reverie.

"You do pretty good work, Coltrane. I guess a lick of paint and it'll be finished."

"Waiting for the weather to dry a bit more, be more stable."

"Weather ever stable here in Wyoming? You know

something I don't know?"

"Nope. Just more optimistic."

"Heck, you must be if you're still expectin' that doctor to come on back."

Shiloh skipped down from the front door and stood back on the boardwalk, admiring his handiwork.

Joe sidled up to him. "Whatcha gonna do with it if she don't return?"

"She'll be back."

Joe shook his head in wonder. "It's like, what, four month now—no, longer, maybe. And you still think she'll be back?"

He turned and met the other man's gaze. "She wouldn't have traveled in all that snow, and it takes about ten days anyways. She'd have got caught out in the train in a drift. She knew that."

Joe laughed. "Well, you got an excuse for everything. I thought Sheriff deputized you or something, someone said."

"Nope."

"But you're not—"

He pivoted around, anger heating him like a strike of lightning. "I'm thinking it through. Waiting to hear what the marshal has to say. I don't see why I should do his job for him, go all that distance down to Colorado and find Yeager when the marshal's right there in Denver."

Joe's forehead lined with thought. "I thought I heard you were hell-bent on revenge for your sister's death and all. And that doctor, the fire and murders."

Shiloh turned back to look up at the house. "I was. I am. But I'm waiting."

"You losing your nerve, Coltrane?"

"I'm not losing any nerve. I'm thinking maybe living is a whole lot better than dying." He ran his gaze over the house, from the roof to the front door. "What color do you think it should be? Maybe a nice blue, huh?"

"Blue's fine." Joe started to move on. "Just don't forget to hang her shingle…and a sign on the door saying, 'The doctor is out.' "

****

Bored out of her mind, Sydney hungered for the usefulness she had felt in Wyoming. Even if some of the townspeople hadn't trusted her medical judgment or capabilities, at the reservation, with all its problems, she had been of some use. And there were times in the town she had been of use. What would the saloon girls be doing now? Who would be treating them? Or the laundresses at the fort? Had she had more time, she was sure she might have won over the town and set up a decent practice.

And then there was Shiloh. His gentle ways, his care. She felt none of that now with Garnforth. If she could come to forgive herself for the killing she had done in self-defense, surely she could forgive Shiloh for protecting other people, their property, their lives, and for going after men who needed to be captured or killed.

Her heart ached.

In love with Garnforth? Could love have died or was it ever there? Was it just some dream, some schoolgirl crush, an infatuation, admiration of something she aspired to? Perhaps she had been more enamored of Iona's accomplishments.

These thoughts crept in with her boredom. She

fixed herself constantly to please him, changed gowns several times a day, conversed with Henshaw over meal planning, and then was considered unpresentable to guests because she wasn't as yet married to Garnforth. It humiliated and disheartened her, made her feel like some prisoner thus far.

She made up her mind.

Garnforth's office at home held the masculine appearance of a doctor's office. Heavy mahogany furniture and an ornate desk that overpowered the room made anyone who presented themselves before him feel small and unimportant. That was how she felt now as she entered after knocking.

He glanced up, surprise and a certain amount of displeasure fleeting across his features before he momentarily bowed his head again to his papers and then gazed at her finally.

"My dear?"

"I…I've come to ask when you think I might get back to work? I was under the impression we were to share an office, patients, and I would be the primary doctor while you taught your classes at the university."

"That was your impression? I am sorry, then, if I gave you that impression. I do not feel we can be seen together in that manner until we are wed." He scrabbled in his drawer and withdrew something as he rose, slipping it into his pocket. "I was also under the impression you had plans to speak to your father."

"Yes, thank you for the money. I shall…send it tomorrow when I am out. I have an appointment tomorrow afternoon with Father."

Garnforth came forward, his arms extended as a smile widened on his lips. "Why, my dear, that is marvelous. Perfectly marvelous. I am sure this whole matter can be straightened out and finalized to everyone's acceptance and pleasure. I am going to gift you Iona's medical bag, to replace the one you lost. And we will set a date for the nuptials. I am sure your father will be happy with that and will gladly extend a donation to the clinic. Once that is done and we are wed, you will, of course, return to work until children come along."

"And after?"

"Oh, my sweet. Let us take one step at a time."

"You seem to have everything—"

"Hush." He put a finger to his lips and smiled, his eyes lighting. "I have a surprise. Well, not exactly a surprise, but I have long been waiting to make our engagement official." He reached into his pocket and pulled out the small velvet box he had taken from his desk. Flipping open the lid with one finger, he extended the box to show her. "This will make it official."

Sydney gasped. She stared down at the sapphire-and-diamond ring he held out.

"I do hope it will fit you."

She struggled for air for a moment. "That...that is Iona's. It was Iona's engagement ring."

"Well, yes." He reached out for her hand and slipped the ring on. "A perfect fit. You see?"

"But...but...it is not right."

"Not right? Why ever not? My late wife has no use for it now. You could hardly expect me to toss it out. And it fits you perfectly. It's as beautiful on you as it was on her."

She swayed for a moment, tried to catch her breath.

"You seem speechless. I know it is far more than

you might have expected after the wilds of Wyoming, but truly, my dear, you are worth every penny."

****

Four side arms and two rifles lay on the table waiting their turn to be oiled and checked. The pair of Colt Peacemakers he had inherited from his father sat next to the Smith and Wesson-3s that had only minutes ago lightened his hips. Two Browning Winchesters, an 1894 and the newer 1895, on which he had spent all the money from a single job, were also there. Shiloh sat, his feet up on the table, staring at them as if they might clean and oil themselves. His gaze was blank, unfocused, but he was all too aware Bones had come in, had clicked the door shut behind him, and was now tugging off his boots, his eyes fixed on his boss.

"That horse you was trainin' this mornin' gonna be a fine cutting horse. You turnin' into quite the rancher." He glanced down at the guns laid out and glanced back to Shiloh. "Maybe all these years you was jus' in the wrong line of business."

Shiloh peered up at the older man, his gaze narrowed, the lines between his eyes deepened. "Yeah." His feet slammed down onto the floor. "Or maybe I'm just getting too damn old for anything else." He started to gather up the firearms and place them back in their cases.

"Too old?" Bones' voice was quiet, thoughtful. He eased himself into a chair at the table. "Son, you have no idea what old is. You how old? Twenty-seven? Twenty-eight? Maybe thirty? You still gots your whole life ahead of you. That woman come back, you get married, settle down, have babies. She don't come back, you find someone else."

Shiloh's hand pounded so hard on the table Bones jumped. "I don't want anyone else." He stood back. "I just…I just…I don't know what the heck got into me. I knew what I was doing before she came along, I knew I was going after Meg's killers, everything was clear. Now nothing is clear. And I'd a thought if Sydney was coming back she'd be back by now. I need to leave for Colorado, but I don't feel I can."

"Ain't your business to go after that man. You asked to be deputized. Sheriff said 'no.' Marshal's business, not yours. If it were anyone else, they'd be leavin' it to the law. Why you think you gotta go on and do that, Boss? Why you think it's your responsibility?"

He slid into the chair once more, facing Bones as if he were facing a jury. "It is my responsibility. You know that. She was my flesh and blood, my kin. No marshal or sheriff is gonna care about getting Yeager the way I do. And no lawman is as good with a gun as I am. You know that. I know that."

"And you think your sister, your Margaret, or Meg as you call her, would want you risking your life to avenge her death?" He waited for an answer, but there was none. "I think not. I truly think not."

Shiloh leaned back in his chair and rocked several times before it came crashing down. He leaned over, almost threatening Bones in his manner. "Thing is, she's not here to tell me. And I think that's just making an excuse."

****

Sydney entered the once-familiar vestibule as the maid stepped aside. She glanced up at the electric portico light, took in there was new carpeting in the hallway, but the same air of quiet rectitude and wealth permeated the silent hall.

"May I take your coat, miss?"

"Of course." Sydney slipped her arms out of the lightweight suit jacket and smoothed her skirt front. She didn't bother to correct the maid as to her title; it would be a useless exercise and bound to annoy her parents if they found out.

"Your father is expecting you, miss." She started to lead the way.

"Is my mother at home? I should like to pay my respects to her first, if I may."

"I'm sorry, miss. Mrs. Cantrell is out for the day. I believe it is her day for open houses."

"I see." She did see: her father would have instructed her mother to make herself unavailable, go on a round of visits. "Well. I shall see my father, then. He is in his office?"

"Yes, miss. Please follow me."

Arthur Cantrell did not rise as his daughter was announced by the maid and lingered in the doorway. He studied her as she stood after the servant had left, careful to close the heavy door quietly behind her. Sydney remained there, waited to be asked in.

He didn't invite her farther, but lashed into his admonishments straight away.

"So. You are living—unwed, I believe—with that doctor or professor or whatever he fancies himself and dare to present yourself here."

"I have recently returned from Wyoming, Father, and have no place else to go, you and Mama being apparently reluctant to house me."

"We will not! I do not recognize you as any daughter of mine. As far as I am concerned, I have no child. You have followed a path of which I do not approve."

"So it would appear. You do not approve of a woman having a career, being a doctor, giving aid to other people, caring for others, doing anything other than—"

His voice boomed. "I do not care for a woman who acts and presents herself as a man, goes to the wilderness of the West, an untamed country, and dresses and—"

"I respectfully remind you, sir, Wyoming is part of the United States. It received its statehood in 1890."

"And gave women the vote. How ridiculous! A barbarous territory, lawless in the extreme. And you, of all people, decide to go there, of all places!"

"Had women doctors been more acceptable here in Philadelphia, I might not have gone. But I dare say I am glad I did. It was a wonderful experience. I found I was of great use, and met many fascinating people. It was a *worthwhile* experience. I wish you could understand that, sir. I wish you could see a time when women will be equal to men, hold the same jobs men do, work—"

"Women cannot do the same jobs men do! They are built differently, have not the same strength, the same firmness of mind. And, dare I remind you, miss, they are made for having babies. *That* is your primary occupation in life. That is what you are built for!"

"Father, I do believe my mind to be equal to any man's. That may be regarded as presumptuous of me, but I did graduate from the medical college, and had I not passed the examinations nor understood the theories and practices of the profession, I would not have the title of Doctor. I wish you could accept that."

"Accept that! I do not need to accept it. Should you wish to be accepted by *me,* you will renounce your so-called profession, decline to practice medicine any more, and marry."

"And I imagine you have someone in mind for my husband as well?"

"You may marry that widower doctor you are living with now. I have no doubt no one else will be interested in you."

But, oh, yes, there was someone else interested in marrying her, if only she could get back, if only she knew if he was still alive, still wanted her.

Her father seemed to gather himself, settled his clasped hands on the desk, and sat back in the towering leather chair that enveloped him.

Someone had once told her in Wyoming that if she ever encountered a bear she should try to make herself look bigger, extend her arms, and growl. She almost laughed, for that was exactly what her father seemed to be doing—trying to make himself look bigger and growling at his opponent, her.

It was with some reluctance she responded to her father, "We intend to marry. We also intend to start a clinic."

"You will continue to practice, then."

There was no way around this. Either she must put forward the request Garnforth had entailed upon her, or the visit was useless—less than useless—for she could see neither her father nor Garnforth would much care for her if this did not go forward.

"Garnforth has…has demanded of me to ask if you might consider donating a sum toward this clinic. He would, of course, put your name on it—that is, name the clinic for you—along with his."

"The impudence of it!" Arthur Cantrell's voice thundered to the point of making several items on shelves in the room shake. "The nerve! He first encourages my daughter, against my wishes, to become a doctor, study and seek a profession, aids you in obtaining a post some two thousand miles away from your family in a wilderness fraught with danger, brings you home to live *contra bonos mores* in his house, and then has the vile idea I might finance his desires for a clinic in which you would no doubt work, and put his name with mine on the building! The very idea! Does it not strike you as odd..." He rose from his seat and came around to the front of the desk. "He asks you to put this to me, and yet he has not as yet set a date for your wedding?"

"It is I who have postponed the marriage. As you see..." She held out her hand with the engagement ring glinting in the chandelier light from above. "He has officially asked for my hand."

"He has not asked *me*!"

Sydney stood immobile, thoughts flying through her brain like ashes on the wind. Garnforth had, indeed, sent her to do his dirty work and had not even requested her hand in marriage with permission from her father. It certainly did not matter to her one iota, but it did strike her as strange he had omitted that tradition while sending her here to request funds from her parent.

"Yes," she said at last. "You are quite right, Father. It is my mistake, and I do beg your pardon." She pivoted away toward the door but faced him once more before she proceeded. "Please give my love and express my regrets to Mother. I doubt either of you will see me again."

In her pocket, she felt the money meant to be wired to Shiloh, but she had another use for it now, a use he would no doubt much prefer.

****

Shiloh straightened out his bedroll on the bed he'd bought for her and left the saddle and his other belongings in the corner. A week ago he had sorted things with Bones. The branding was finished, and the old man hopefully only had the summer to get through with help from Bates and maybe one or two others. Their parting conversation had been subdued, which was pretty much how Shiloh felt. Now, he walked through the house, the Doctor's Office sign whining as it swayed in the wind, creaking a ghostly sigh.

She hadn't come back.

He would take it down in the morning and wire the Title Division of Wyoming State to put the property for sale. Or maybe he should keep it as a townhouse, get someone to run it as a hostelry. Maybe a decision was best left 'til he returned.

If he returned.

Outside, the train whistle wailed its mournful cry. Tomorrow he'd load up Whiskey and his pack mule and be on his way down to Cheyenne.

Chapter Thirteen

Sydney stepped down off the train into the chill of a Wyoming night; the cold masked her face and made her shiver for a moment. She hadn't expected this in late spring, but she was wrapped in the coat Shiloh had bought her, and the dress as well, meant for winter. All the clothes purchased on Iona's accounts had been neatly stacked on her bed, while the engagement ring topped the pile along with a note that simply read, *"Garnforth, I am so sorry. I cannot marry you. I am returning west. Perhaps without my involvement Father will reconsider a possible investment in your clinic. I am indebted to you for your help in my education. I truly wish you much success and future happiness, Sydney."*

Tired beyond thought after the long journey, she picked up the medical bag Garnforth had gifted to her, along with the small satchel containing the few personal items Shiloh had purchased for her when she left. She listened to the retreating cry of the train as it moved on toward Utah and beyond, and dragged her feet down the platform toward the center of town, uncertain as to what her future held. Even this first night was so indefinite—should she go into the saloon and ask for a corner there, or should she make her way to the livery stable and either take a space there or rent a horse to try to get out to Shiloh's ranch—if she could find her way in the dark.

The dark. Almost midnight and nary a light was lit in the shops and houses of the town. Only some music floated out on the night wind as if it beckoned her to make the decision to go into the saloon. Madam Collette would recognize her and perhaps give her board for one night. Perhaps.

The shuttered windows and darkened interiors made her feel more alone than at any other time in her life. One after another, she trudged by shops, lifeless and obscured. A cat jumped from one overhang to another, a momentary mewing giving Sydney a shiver. If only she had arrived in daylight with people around, people who might recognize her, possibly welcome her back, offer her help.

The saloon was dark except for dim light showing through a curtain from the top floor, and the soft tinkling of a piano in the upstairs brothel with an occasional giggle. Sydney noted the front window had been repaired, no longer boarded up, as it had been when she left. She decided she had no choice but to see if she might stay here; it was her best bet. Knocking lightly on the inner doors, now locked, she waited to see if the person or persons awake upstairs might come to her aid.

A second, stronger knock brought a response.

Madam Collette stuck her head out the upstairs window. "Go away, we're closed, whoever you are!"

Sydney stepped back off the boardwalk and peered up at the madam.

"Good grief! Is that you, Doc?"

"I'm afraid it is. I'm so sorry to disturb you, but—"

"Stay there. I'll be right down."

Within a few moments, the door squeaked open and Madam Collette stood holding her wrapper closed, motioning Sydney inside. "Well, look who the cat brought in. Never thought I'd be seeing you again."

"No, it's been a while. I'm sorry to be bothering you this late—"

"Oh, it ain't late for me. Charley and I was just...having a little fun."

"I heard the piano music and thought...well, I really have no place else to go this time of night. I just stepped off the train and thought it would have to be here or the stables, and then I heard—"

"No place else to go? Guess you haven't seen. Hasn't Coltrane been writing to you, then? Don't you know?"

A chill went through her at the mention of Shiloh's name. How she had missed him, how stupid had she been trying to deny she was in love with him?

"Know what? No, we haven't been in touch. I...I tried...well, I told him it would be best if we didn't write."

"Well." Collette shook her head at the mystery. "He may not have written, but he sure did build."

"Build?"

"We all been calling it Coltrane's Folly."

Sydney's face scrunched in lack of understanding. "I see he fixed the saloon window. Is that what you mean?"

"Oh, goodness, no, love. He's gone and built you offices right here in the middle of town, offices and accommodation upstairs, I understand, though I never been over to see it myself."

Her lips could hardly form the word, "What?"

153

"Kept telling everyone hereabouts you was comin' back, like he knowed it for a fact. Insisted. Spent every fine day he could spare coming right into town and working on it. Any day in the winter, snow permitting and all, then he finished it off soon as spring appeared. As I say, I haven't been over, but Joe down at the mill tells me it's as fine a construction as he's ever seen. We all knew Coltrane was good with his hands that way."

Sydney stood dumbfounded.

"'Course, we never believed you would come back. It's been months and all, but he was insistent."

Speechless, Sydney looked around for a chair to collapse into.

"Here. You best have some tea or something. I can fetch it, and then maybe you want to see if that house is unlocked. You may be more comfortable there than here with, you know, the goings on and all—not that you're not welcome, of course."

"No, no, of course. I didn't mean to bother you. I...I think I'll just go over and maybe stop in here, in the morning."

Madam Collette did not pretend to want to hold her back. She stepped out on the boardwalk past Sydney and pointed down the street. "There it is, love. See the shingle and all he has hanging out? You go have a look, and if it's locked or something, you come on back here. I'll wait a minute or two, just in case."

Sydney collected her bags once more and traipsed down the wooden planks in the direction Collette had pointed. She crossed the silent street, no horses or carts to dodge at this time of night, and stood before the house with the shingle hanging outside. She tried the door.

154

It opened. She dropped the bags inside, stepped to the curb, and waved her good-bye to Collette.

****

Shiloh shook awake, his hand finding the grip of his Smith and Wesson, his finger on the trigger. As the door creaked shut, he lay and listened to the tread of someone entering, dropping bags, a lightness of step as the person stood momentarily, before proceeding to inspect the downstairs. And he knew he could release the firearm.

He knew.

He sat up, leaning back against the headboard of the bed, heeding each step, each stop, each cupboard door that opened, each room door that closed downstairs. This was what he had waited for all these months. He thought if his heart beat any faster, he would need her medical attention before anything else. Impatience streamed through his veins like wildfire through dry brush and, at last, he pulled himself up, yanked his denims on, and strode carefully toward the stairs, barefoot and silent.

Sydney sat on the top step, her back to him, curled over, her arms crossed against her chest, her head bowed. He could tell she was weeping from the little shakes and snivels, holding herself in the peace of the night as if she might wake someone.

He reached out and clasped her shoulder with the lightest touch possible, felt the jolt of surprise before she turned into his waiting arms and let the sobs come full force.

Shiloh'd never been so happy in his life.

He sat beside her on the top step leading from the offices up to the living accommodation. His long legs stretched out, landing three steps down, while her legs were tucked up, her head rested against his chest, his arm around her, his chin nestled in her hair. She had stopped crying now, but words continued to fail her; a sense of comfort and succor replaced the long, lonely months she had spent in Garnforth's company.

At last, she said, "How...how did you know I would come back?"

She could feel him shift slightly, his head come up before it rested once more against her.

"I don't know. I just knew, I just felt it. I thought...I know it sounds silly but it's true...I just felt I loved you so much it had to be true. And then there had never been any sign you were in love with someone else, no...no sort of elation when you read that letter before you told me you were to be wed. It was more as if you felt a duty, and I just didn't believe you could marry someone you didn't love."

"No. And I was so wrong about him. And about you."

"In what way?"

"He didn't love me. Or maybe he did in his own way, but it wasn't what I wanted, needed. And he used me. He wanted my father to donate money to a clinic he thought to build—*that* was his main interest. And he saw me as some sort of replacement for his first wife. I wanted something else." She hesitated. "I wanted you. All along it was right in front of me and I didn't know it. I wanted you, Shiloh."

"Killings and all?"

"When I felt able to forgive myself, I felt I could forgive you, if there was ever anything to forgive. I know I couldn't live with you if you continued, but you haven't, have you? You won't, will you?"

Shiloh sat back somewhat away from her and didn't answer. "I... The sheriff's given up, but the marshal down in Denver is supposedly searching for Yeager."

She pulled away and gazed up into his face, the face she had missed so much all these months, longed to see. "What will you do?"

"Wait. Now you're back, I'll wait. I guess."

She nestled back against him now, the longing overcoming her, the desire. She had never known she could want a man so much, yearn for that completion a man offered, the fulfillment. Was this what love was? The hunger for him was almost more than she could withstand.

She hugged her arms about his waist and rubbed her head against his chest as he nuzzled into her. With gentle care, he clutched her arms and drew her hands into his, enveloping them in his own as his gaze sought her response. She loved those hands, the callouses and tough leather of them, the long fingers with which she now entwined her own.

Shiloh came forward and brushed his lips against her mouth, and Sydney thought she would faint with desire, her breath more a gasp. She opened her mouth to him, let him take control, let the kiss go deep. She hadn't known a kiss could be so overpowering, so all-consuming, take over her entire body as it seemed to yield to him. She couldn't help herself but ran her hands over his bare back and chest, felt the solidness, the rock-hard muscles of his upper arms as her fingers traveled back down to his hands.

She hadn't been allowed to read certain parts the

male medical students were permitted, nor had she seen certain parts of the anatomy books, but she thought she knew what to expect physically. Yet anatomy lessons were not in her mind as Shiloh lifted her into his arms, his lips and tongue taking possession of her as she lost herself to him.

She felt weightless, light, as if the kiss sent fire right down to her toes, and she had to grip his shoulders so as not to become totally limp in his grasp.

Shiloh stood with her, turned with care on the stairs, and stepped up to the top. He pulled his kiss away and locked his gaze with hers.

"You haven't seen the upstairs yet."

"No."

Adjusting his grip on her, he gave her that half-smile she had come to love.

"Want to do that now?"

"Only the bedroom, please."

His smile widened and lit his face. She had never seen him smile like that, that broad.

She laughed.

In the bedroom, he set her down and, with the most careful, slow movements, took the pins out of her hair, one by one, and laid them on a dresser he had bought for her. As he did so, the lengths of gold hair fell about her shoulders, and he thought she looked other-worldly, like some princess from a storybook. He ran his fingers through the silken strands, gathered her face to him once more, and waited for her mouth to receive him. His body was growing impatient, requesting the blue jeans be removed, but he waited to unbutton Sydney's shirtwaist. The ache between his legs would get worse, but he wanted this to be a night she would not forget, not one whose meaning he would neglect. This was not only a consummation of physical need but a consummation of their love, something he believed would last forever.

When her hair was down, he noted how young she looked, how chaste and pure. He had never taken a woman like that; his previous encounters had been with women of dubious backgrounds, or those all too ready to give themselves to him without a thought to the relationship. But here was Sydney, who had shown how much she loved him, who cared, who was different. And she was his. Or going to be, willing to be.

His hand shook slightly as he moved a length of hair out of her face and moved in for another kiss as he finally reached behind her to undo the buttons of her shirtwaist. Part of him wanted to hurry, yet another part of him wanted to linger, savor her, remember every single step they took together this night.

As he found the last button, he stood back for a moment, then tenderly pulled the blouse forward, exposing her corset and the skin above her breasts. He ran his fingers over her shoulders, felt the satin.

"Oh, lord, you're so beautiful, Sydney. So very beautiful."

She smiled up at him and slowly pivoted for him to undo the corset laces. His hands continued to shake, but he pulled the laces free and threw the corset aside, waited a moment to turn her toward him.

He gasped.

He thought he had never seen such a beautiful woman, the firm uplift of her breasts, the way her rib cage narrowed down to her waist, the gold hair.

Sydney released her skirt and petticoats herself and

stepped out of them, pushed her stockings down in front of him after she had removed her button-up shoes. She reached for the metal buttons of his blue jeans, knowing as she undid them she would release his manhood, but he clasped her hands once more.

"You...you get into bed," he advised.

She nodded her head in consent and sat on the edge of the bed, removed her pantaloons, let them drop to the floor before lying back against the bedroll that was spread out on the bed, nervously covered herself with the blankets there. She peeked over the top as Shiloh undressed, didn't make a show of himself but pushed the jeans to the floor, and twisted and sat on the bed as he released himself. He kicked the legs of the pants away before he swiveled to face her. Her gaze was on him, a slight grin as she watched him crawl in beside her, scoop her into his arms once more, hold her against his chest.

The feel of her skin against him overwhelmed him. There was nothing like it, to feel so close to another human being, no covering, not a thing between them. He pulled her on top to feel her breasts rest against him as he moved his hand up the side of her face and pulled her close once more.

Sydney knew what to expect and yet didn't. She had read regarding the mechanics of the act as if humans were some automated machines that simply acted in a certain way in order to produce children. "A man has needs," had been one of the statements of her anatomy professor, but there had never been anything regarding what a woman's needs might be, or even if she had any. But now, she knew. She knew she needed Shiloh, she needed his touch, his kiss, the weight of his body on hers, the feel of his hands as they moved over her breasts, massaged the nipples, and found the center of her being. She needed him inside her, the movement, his breath in her ear. She needed to know he loved her, he needed her as much as she needed him, he wanted her as much as she wanted him, and this was not some random act of lust to simply satisfy his "needs."

And she found that. And more.

He was patient with her, slow, unaware of the hunger within her. His touch was careful, caring, yet it ignited her with a longing for more. His lips found a spot on her neck that did something to her no medical book could have described. She tried to pleasure him but lost herself, all thoughts cleared from her mind as she acted and reacted without a sense of what she was doing or how she was doing it or the time passing.

Her senses were more alive than they had ever been, as if everything she consisted of was held within those acknowledgements. She tasted the salt from his skin, the sweetness of his mouth. Felt the rough fingertips travel over her as if she were a roadmap to his heart. Heard his heartbeat, his sighs and moans, voiced her own. And saw in her mind's eye their future together, the future they could build here in Wyoming.

When she could stand it no more, could not continue without him completing her, she felt the momentary pain as he laid his final claim to her, moved within her and took her to a new realm of sensation, all senses lost to this one moment.

She didn't know how much time had passed when she shifted slightly under Shiloh's weight and he rose up on his elbows and pecked her first on her mouth, then let his tongue travel between her breasts, licking a line of sweat before he kissed her again. She entwined her fingers in his disheveled hair and pulled him in to her for a proper, deep kiss before she released him to rest against her, the way she fell asleep with him, entangled.

Chapter Fourteen

She awoke to sunshine brightening the room, the sound of clattering pans somewhere a short distance from her, the sense of loss of his company in the bed, the weight gone, the touch no longer present. She stretched lazily, wondered at the miracle that had transpired, in awe of herself for being so completely happy. After a life of pleasing others, her parents, the Willises—especially Garnforth—and other professors and teachers, she had a feeling her life ahead would be one of mutual love and care.

Shiloh leant in the doorway, his jeans on, his chest bare, that grin upon his face. "You dreaming?"

"Uh-hmmm." She smiled at him, shy over the intimacy but reveling in the fact. She took in the hard lines of muscle across his stomach, the light mat of hair on his chest, and the trail from his navel.

He came to her, crawled up the bed in one movement, and grabbed her for a kiss. He squatted back but didn't let her go. "Breakfast is ready. If you're hungry."

"Starved."

Her gaze couldn't release him. For a man, he was beautiful rather than handsome, the gray of his eyes like a sky before the peace of snow, the promise of quiet. Yet there was always something more, something tough and unrelenting she could spend her life trying to understand.

"Well, then?" The half smile again as he swirled around and sprang off the bed. "You've got five minutes."

"Five minutes?"

"Five."

She left off the corset, dressed as if there had been an emergency, washed, and went toward the sounds of his efforts, the clamor of cooking.

"It won't be great. Bones does the cooking at the ranch."

"So I noticed."

"Well, I guess it's edible."

She pulled out a chair at a small table with four places and let herself be served, catered to. Fatigue from last night mingled with the exhaustion of the journey caught her unawares. Shiloh served up eggs, a pile of bread, coffee. For a while, she just cast him the occasional smile, received one before he ducked his head again to his plate and ate. She felt a quiet comfort but something else as well, a tension, something he was holding back.

When he finished, he pushed his chair back a bit and gazed across at her.

"I still can't believe you came back."

"But you said you knew I would."

"I did. I believed it. But then I sort of gave up." He seemed to wait for a reply, but she finished her meal and sat, stared back at him. He reached across for her hand. "I have…I have to tell you something."

Sydney felt a sudden chill and took back her hand, wrapped her arms around herself, cradled herself against his words.

"I haven't told you the whole truth. About Yeager. About my intentions."

"Oh, no, Shiloh. No." She rocked herself as if comfort would come from the act.

"It's all right," he started. "I won't go now. But I wanted you to know the truth. When you hadn't come back and all...I had given up on you, and I know where Yeager is. I had to wait out the winter because I'd never have made it through the Rockies. He's hiding in a place called Estes Park. In Colorado."

"But you can wire the sheriff or the marshal down there. They'll get him." She heard the plea in her voice.

"Maybe. For now. I'll wire the marshal, tell him what I know, and wait. Sheriff said the marshal was going after Yeager. I'd brought all my guns, ready to go, and I would have if you hadn't arrived. You should know that. And you should know if he isn't successful I *will* go, Syd. I will. Because until this is finished I'll never rest easy."

"And the ranch?"

"Bones is there. He's worked with cattle almost his whole life, and he knows what to do, and is honest. He's a good man."

"It wasn't Bones who asked me once to marry him."

"No." He bit his lip. "And if I asked you again now?"

She laid down her fork and glanced away. Outside, as the town awoke, there were the sounds of carriage wheels, the vibrations from the boardwalk below, some shouts of greeting, a dog barking. She looked around and knew how much he must love her; the evidence was right here, the thought that had gone into this building, the care, even to the extent of fitting it out as best he could, thinking what she might need to begin with. Such an expression of love. No one had ever loved her that much, shown such care for her.

And yet she felt to marry him was condoning killing, went against everything she believed. How could a man who was so gentle and kind, so caring, also be so deadly, a killer?

She took a deep breath and met his gaze. "Shiloh. I cannot answer now. You have to understand. I do love you. I do. But I don't love what you seem to be—"

"A rancher?" He gave that half smile.

"You know what I mean."

"Sorry. Yes. But, Sydney, you're only seeing one side of me. You're—"

"No! No, that is why this is so very difficult. I believe I see you as someone who is kind and caring and loving, but then there is this other side I cannot abide. I cannot live with someone who intends to kill."

"I haven't any intentions of that. At the moment."

She sat back and studied him. "I'm too tired...after last night...to make any kind of decision that affects both our lives forever. And I do not want to make the wrong decision."

"You love me?"

"Yes."

"Then I don't see what decision there is to make."

"You want me to stand by you if you go off and kill this man?"

"I want you to understand some men need killing, some men cannot be left to roam and kill again. *He's* the killer, Syd, not me." He tapped his finger on the table several times, obviously deep in thought or reluctant to tell her what was in front of her. "You killed, Syd. I hate to remind you of it. In self defense. Can you not consider killing Yeager self-defense as well?"

"But it's not!"

"Defense of those he will go on to kill, defense of my sister and nephew who cannot defend themselves!"

She sat back and held her head, shaking, trying to deny what was right in front of her. Confusion is what she felt above everything, exhaustion from trying to sort out her feelings, and love for this man.

****

Shiloh gathered up his firearms and saddle from the bedroom and moved them into a back room, the use of which he had left to Sydney's decision. She could make it a sitting room or a spare bedroom or whatever she liked. From downstairs came the sound of her opening cupboards and inspecting the contents, the medicines and other items he had ordered for her. She would no doubt want to order more, but what went through his mind now was whether the town would accept her, and more importantly, if he stayed here, what they would make of the relationship without them being married. He didn't want her to have more problems at settling into her life here than she already had.

He could hear the tired steps mounting the stairs and faced the doorway just as she appeared.

"I've made a list, some other items I should have on hand, but you've done remarkably well. How did you know what to order?"

"Rode over to the rez. Asked that new doctor what he would want to have on hand, and ordered double of everything."

Her mouth opened and shut again. "That was...remarkably generous of you."

"It wasn't much. I knew it would be what you'd want, for them to have the medicines as well as the town."

She raised her arms as if to embrace him but stayed where she was. "You are so good, such a very fine man, Shiloh."

"And yet..."

"No, please don't bring it up again. Please. Not right now."

"Have you considered yet what the town will say if I stay? If we have a child. Unwed."

"Of course that is something I am thinking of. But marriage is permanent. I don't want to tie you to me if I...if I cannot abide your ways."

"You'd rather have a child out of wedlock? Even now you may...you may be carrying." He realized he had a spark of hope somewhere inside of him.

"I'm well aware of the problems, the possibilities."

"Do you want me to go? Perhaps it'd be best. For now."

"I...I no longer know what I want." She pivoted back into the kitchen and collapsed into a chair. "This is your house, your work, I don't feel I can dictate—"

"No, it's yours. I built it all for you, bought everything for you. A wedding gift, I thought."

Her face tilted up to him. "What about the ranch?"

"I didn't figure things out yet, thought it best to discuss with you. I can't be sitting here doing nothing while you and Bones both work. 'Course, as I said, Bones is reliable and all, but I can't leave it all to him indefinitely. He's getting on in age, and I have to look ahead. There's talk of them new telephones coming in here, and I thought we could have them, but of course the patients would have to have access to one as well." He stopped in his plans, thought. "Some folks are closer to the ranch than town, you know that."

"Shiloh." She took a deep breath, rested her hand on the table, drummed her fingers for several seconds. "I think we must let this play out, you must give me time to see what I feel. I know I love you, but it would be foolish…for either of us…to rush into a marriage that may end up unhappy for either or both."

"I could never be unhappy with you. Even if you hated me for what I am, I would still love you."

"You say that now, but I doubt it is so."

"So shall I stay for now? Or leave?"

"Stay. Please stay."

In the afternoon, she walked with him, her arm looped through his as a couple would. He tapped his Stetson to ladies as they passed, Sydney proud to be seen with him now, though some of the glances they received were less than friendly. On occasion, she received a "Welcome back," which gladdened her heart.

"I need to stop in and thank Madam Collette for her help last night. She was the one who told me you had built the house."

"I'm not a favorite with her, but all right."

"How can you not be a favorite?"

"I told you—I don't make use of the upstairs, so I'm not a paying customer."

Sydney had to wonder what Collette would make of her now she would know Shiloh had been at the house all night.

"Perhaps we'll leave it then, if you prefer."

"No. I didn't say that. 'Sides which, don't you see to the girls? Best to pay your respects, then."

"Yes, of course. If I have no other patients, at least I might continue to have them."

Shiloh pushed open the saloon door, the lively music enveloping them.

"Well, look what the cat dragged in." Bozy wiped down his bar, wrung out his cloth in a basin of water, and wiped once more.

Shiloh caressed her hand, smirked at Bozy. "Nice window you got out there. So clean you'd think it was new."

Bozy leant on the bar. "It is clean. It is new. Let's keep it that way." He stood back. "How you like your new office and house he built ya, Doc? Shiloh'd make quite a living building round these parts if he set his mind to. You gonna put the lot of us to shame with such a fine building."

"I know. Shiloh did a wonderful job. It was a great surprise." She waited a beat before asking, "Is Madam Collette awake and about as yet? I'd like a word."

"You gonna be doctoring again? I heared they got a new one up at the rez."

"Yes, they have, but the town hasn't a doctor yet, has it? I had some patients before, when I had the room at the mercantile."

"Well. Guess some folks might not be picky about who looks down 'em; me, I won't be one to discuss my private matters with a lady."

"Yet you're no doubt one who would gladly send his wife to discuss her private matters with a man."

"Well, that's the way of it, isn't it? Or you expectin' to have all female patients like the doves?"

"I'm expecting to make myself useful wherever I'm needed and with whomever may need and want me."

Bozy snorted. "Well, go on up then, 'cause they sure as hell need ya."

She squeezed Shiloh's hand and mounted the stairs without him. There were some giggles from behind closed doors, but she suspected it was more likely to be girl talk rather than early goings-on. She knocked at Madam Collette's door and got a shout to enter.

The room was draped in red velvet with gold trimmings, heavy worn furniture almost filling the space. A big brass bed was the centerpiece, but there were chairs and the piano she had heard last night, a table set with a vase of flowers.

"Well, well. I guess you got in last night."

"I did. Thank you."

"Was Shiloh still there?"

"Yes, yes, he was. How did you know?"

Collette seemed to glide off the bed on which she'd been lying, a filmy light wrapper of some nature floating behind. She pulled the tie tighter to make the closure more respectable, though it didn't do much where her breasts were concerned.

Sydney tried not to look away.

"He'd been in town. Saw him about. Bozy said he was headed down to Colorado. That so?"

"He had been. He's...he's staying put for a while."

"I bet he is." Collette plonked herself against the table. "So, you're back. Same deal as before?"

"Of course. I appreciate that, Collette."

171

"I don't know if you'll appreciate what the other ladies in town will think of it."

"They don't think much of me anyway. At least that's the impression I get. So it won't make much difference. Still, I didn't do too badly before. Out on the farms and ranches people seem to be a little less fussy. And I had plenty to eat." She turned back to clasp the doorknob. "You don't like Shiloh, he said. Is that because he isn't a customer or something else?"

"Something else." Collette sealed her lips and glanced away.

"But you're not going to tell me."

"You never met his sister, I guess."

"No. I believe she was killed some time before I arrived, some time before I met Shiloh."

"Yes. She was a saint, that woman, never saw me or the girls as any different from her. Rather like yourself, I guess. At least so I think. Always doing charitable work, bringing things we might need, talking to the girls like a friend. And Shiloh, he'd gone off, doing his own thing, hiring himself out, you might say, defending others so far as I know, but for sale. When he shoulda been here on that ranch that night defending her."

"But...she married Parmeter. Did you ever meet him, ever think that was strange?"

"'Course I met him, 'course we all thought it was strange, a woman like that and a man like Parmeter, a no-good, you could tell right off. But he was a sweet talker and she was lonely, I guess. Listen, who am I to speechify I understand love. I understand sex, is all. But love? Love is blind, as they say, blind as a bat."

****

172

She was preparing their dinner a couple of hours later when the banging on the front door was swiftly followed by one of the locals barging in and shouting.

"Doc, Doc, come quick. Bozy's just dropped down on the floor, dead as a door nail. Come quick!"

Chapter Fifteen

Kneeling by him, she felt for the pulse in his neck. Faint, very faint. She leant over him to see if there was breath. A hint. She immediately loosened his collar and started chest compressions, counting to herself, praying as well. She kept her hands crossed on Bozy's chest, pushing down hard and releasing before starting again, oblivious to the group gathering around her, catching Shiloh's perplexed face out of the corner of her eye.

Suddenly Bozy jolted up and started coughing. Sydney sat back.

There was a general gasp and mutterings all around as she took Bozy's hand and felt his pulse, counting against Iona's watch on a brooch that hung from her chest.

When she was satisfied, Sydney reached in her bag and shook out a vial. "Let's get this under your tongue, please." She kept her voice calm, soft, as Bozy opened his mouth and she filled the dropper. She let a drop of the tincture go into his mouth.

"What…what happened?"

"You passed out, had a heart attack of some nature, I believe."

"A heart attack…why would I have a heart attack?"

Sydney sat back on her haunches and smiled down at him. "Do you have any pain in your chest?

Tightness? Difficulty breathing?"

"A little tightness, I guess. Like something sitting on me."

She shook her head in compliance. "I'm prescribing bed rest for a while, and digitalis. That should help." She looked around. "Can someone help him home, please? With care."

One of the men stepped forward and pointed at her. "You brought him back to life. Just like that. I wouldn't have believed it if I hadn't seen with my own eyes. He was dead, and now he's alive."

Bozy tried to look up at the men, then back to her.

Sydney stood, the circle of men all dumbfounded, as if they'd seen a miracle.

She reached once more into her bag and brought out the vial of tincture. "Can two of you help him home, please," she repeated. "He needs to stay in bed until the tightness eases." She glanced at Shiloh, pleading. "Please."

Shiloh's gaze took in the group. "Mason, you and I can chair-lift him over to his quarters. We're about the biggest. Let's see if we can get him up and on our crossed hands with his arms around our necks."

****

He stepped out from Bozy's house, nodding his farewell and thanks to Mason before heading back to the doctor's office. He was overcome with love for Sydney, and so proud of what she had just done. Amazed. He felt elated, just knowing she had said she loved him as well. But now his main concern was trying to make her understand his stance regarding his sister's killer. He knew she truly loved him; she had said as much, yet she remained unwilling or unable to accept his belief what he had done in the past was right, and what he might have to do in the future was the proper thing to do.

A warm wind blew, and he pulled his hat down to protect his eyes from the dust; his boots sounded on the wooden boardwalk. He was suddenly aware of the hastening jingle of spurs behind as if someone was coming up to surprise him, and he flipped around in a single motion, his Smith and Wesson-3 already drawn.

"Hold up, Coltrane, for chrissake." Dan Fry, the sheriff's deputy, stood stock still, his hands in the air. "Sheriff sent me to get ya. Heard over at the saloon you'd been in and taken Bozy home, so I come after you."

Shiloh holstered his gun and stared at Fry as the man lowered his hands. "What the heck does the sheriff want now?"

"Help, I think." Fry stood there, peering over at Shiloh as if he were something lethal and would explode. "He didn't say, but he was moaning over a telegram he just received."

A chill started to creep up Shiloh's spine. He stood helpless for a moment, his dream of proving to Sydney he could live peaceably without going after any more killers fading fast. He had a terrible feeling what that telegram might say. If it had been good news, that Yeager was caught, the sheriff wouldn't be moaning. If the sheriff was upset at the news it had brought, as Dan Fry seemed to imply, it certainly wasn't going to be good news for Shiloh. He motioned to Fry he was following, and the two men headed back to the sheriff's office, Fry keeping off to the side away from him.

The deputy pushed open the door to the office and

immediately made himself scarce at the rear desk.

Sheriff Barnes glanced up, then sat back in his chair, and flicked through some papers. He appeared older, worn, as he held out the dull yellow telegram for Shiloh to read.

"Marshal's dead. Telegram doesn't say anything more than 'Marshal dead, Yeager at large.' I presume Yeager got him. Thought you should know." His gaze met Shiloh's and his eyes widened in query.

"I can read, Sheriff. So you want me to go after him."

"I didn't say that, did I? I have no jurisdiction down there, and—"

"Neither do I. You refused to deputize me, as well. If you don't have jurisdiction, neither do I. I'd just be a gun looking for Yeager."

Sheriff Barnes leaned low across his desk, his hands clasped, squeezing each other, releasing, a nervous movement. For a moment he didn't look up at Shiloh, just tapped the desk. "There's a bounty now. For him killing a US marshal. And it'll be a while before another man comes out to that post."

"So you think I should just make myself useful, go kill Yeager, and get the bounty?"

Barnes wheezed in a breath and sat back in his chair, rocked a bit farther, and kept his gaze on Shiloh. "This is what you wanted, son, this is what you asked for. Your sister's killer. I'm just telling you, it seems to be now or never. Yeager will never stop killing, though he may be expecting someone to be after him now, what with the bounty. It's when and who that is that'll surprise him."

"You think he's not expecting me? You think he

doesn't know I want his hide, that news of Parmeter's death hasn't reached him?"

"I don't think any of that. If *I* know it all, maybe he does. But you came to me and wanted to go after him. So now what's happened?"

He stood wondering if the sheriff would understand anything about what had happened. Love had happened, that's what. But didn't he love his sister—not the same way, of course, but didn't he have a duty to her? It was going to be difficult—nearly impossible—to try to explain this to Sydney now, but he knew very well he must. It was now or never. The time to stop procrastinating had finally come, caught up with him, marched right into his cozy little world of the ranch, the doctor's house, Sydney, and his dream of married life with kids. Would any of it be waiting for him when he got back? He guessed he'd find out.

****

When he opened the door to the doctor's office, the front room he had designed as a waiting room was full. Benches along the wall were crowded, mostly with men, of course, but a few of the younger, more enlightened women were waiting there as well. Several cowhands leant against the wall. To his reckoning, it would be a long day for Sydney, and he wasn't going to have a chance to talk with her in private and explain to her until evening. He'd leave at first light in the morning, after a last night together, one in which, he hoped, she'd stay with him, or rather let him stay with her.

Sydney came out of the examining room, said her farewells to a patient who nodded his head in agreement and clutched a bottle. Shiloh caught her eye as the patient left, before she extended her hand toward the next one in greeting and showed the patient inside. He felt all gazes set on him, their summation of his presence, their thoughts as to his being there, and their estimation of him. He could, of course, be there just checking on something he'd built, but that didn't seem to be the general assessment, he felt.

Later, over supper, he said, "We need to get married, Syd. I see the way folks are looking at me, as if it's my fault, like I'm taking advantage of you and all. They blame me when I'm the one happy to get wed as soon as possible. Tomorrow, in fact."

There was the rise and fall of her chest, a breath in annoyance, before she answered, "I don't think they're blaming you. They're just not condoning, or at least not happy, with you being here. They're not sure exactly what is happening. They know you built this house for me, and now we both seem to be here."

"Seem to be!" He tried to get hold of his frustration, anger. "They know dang well I'm here and you're here. What does that spell? You may have the patients now on the news of what you did for Bozy, but you know that won't last long unless we're wed. Their disapproval will come back, and with that, they'll all leave." He pushed his chair back from the table. "Sheriff got a telegram today. Yeager's killed the marshal down in Colorado."

Her fork was halfway to her mouth when it stopped. "And?"

He rubbed his forehead, his eyes shut. "If I go and you're with child, it will be worse for you."

"If you go, and I'm with child or without child, either way, I will leave. I will set up somewhere else.

179

You know that. I've said that."

He collapsed back against his chair. "You'd let Yeager go on killing. It's that easy for you, is it?"

She slammed the table so vehemently the plates jumped. "Why does it have to be you? Why? I still don't understand that. There will be another marshal, or another sheriff. You don't have to do this!"

"That's where you're wrong, Syd. I do." He stood and came around the table to her, knelt in front of her, and reached up to push a curl back. He could feel her quiver at his touch, saw her eyes well and tears start their trail down her face. He pushed one aside and brought her forward to kiss, patient for her to give in to him, open her mouth to him and let the kiss go deeper.

Then he pulled her into his arms and carried her to the bedroom.

In the morning, sated from lovemaking, entwined like vines on a branch, she felt his breath against her face, the soft kiss to her cheek, and his gentle hand as it pushed strands of hair from her forehead. He began to pull away with care, no doubt trying not to disturb her. Somnolent, she lay unable to open her eyes but sensed his leaving. She felt bereft, betrayed. Sounds reached her of him dressing, pulling his clothes on, buckling his belts, before there was the click of the knob. As she lay back against the pillows she heard him in the other room, gathering his guns, his saddle, and listened as his spurs rang with every step of his descent to the front door.

She couldn't call out, couldn't say farewell or wish him luck. To her it was ending, their relationship; it was going to be finished now.

She towed herself from the bed they had shared

and went to the window, pulled back the curtain with care, and stood to the side to look down out the front. In a short time, he appeared leading his horse, now saddled, with bedroll, and a mule packed with provisions, spare guns. Shiloh checked over everything one last time and then twisted to peer up at the window. Their gazes locked, but neither moved until at last, with no further acknowledgement of her other than a tap to his Stetson, he mounted up and let the animals walk on out of town.

She let the curtain go, fluttering back to cover the window as she stood against the wall, rested her head back. The perfidy she felt was so disturbing to her, she was certain her insides were empty; she was nothing more than a silhouette of her being. And yet, it wasn't treachery or duplicity—he had told her his intentions, explained his reasoning, his needs. Told her all along, right from the beginning.

But could she live with them? Live with herself if she gave in from her own moral standpoint? That was the question.

And it would have to wait a very long time before that question could be answered.

Part Three — Chapter Sixteen

It was two weeks before Shiloh made his way down the arduous trails to Cheyenne, time enough to ask himself numerous questions. Was he doing this to prove a point or was he doing it because he truly felt he had to revenge his sister's death and take Yeager off the map? Or could it possibly be that somewhere inside him he felt he had to make his own stand as a man, as much as he loved Sydney, be true to who he was and stand up to this strong woman?

He felt all of it.

At times, he tried not to think of this or what he was about to do, or the possibility of never seeing her again, either because she would leave or because he'd be killed. He tried to conjure her, think of her kindness, her love, the feel of her skin next to him. Something inside him simply could not accept she would leave him. He envisioned her waiting for him, standing at the ranch doorway smiling, open-armed, happy to see him return.

Situated on the main transcontinental rail line, Cheyenne was quite the bustling metropolis after the quiet of northern Wyoming and small-town life. It seemed, as he rode into town, there were more people here than he'd seen in one place in a very long time. He found a livery with a good farrier to check Whiskey's shoes and a good hotel for himself. It was his first night in civilization, as he thought it, for some while. He couldn't get away fast enough.

A bath, provisions, and an extra supply of .44 cartridges for both the Colts and the Smith and Wessons he carried, as well as the .40-72s for the Winchester rifles, and then Shiloh was crossing into Colorado one day later.

He'd had jobs in Boulder and Denver a few years back, early on in his so-called career. Now he wondered how he'd ever got into this line of work anyway. Good with a gun? Yes, certainly, but so were many others his age. Nerves of steel? Yes, except when it had come to Sydney. Or was he lying to himself? When he had got back to the ranch after so many years as a hired gun, sick of the killing, sick and bored of taking orders from other men, of seeing men die for reasons that might have been sorted by other means than a killing, the last thing he had expected was to be faced with his own good reason to kill again. It seemed unfair. But then, life was unfair, as his father had repeatedly pointed out to him. Had he been lazy in his youth, or had he just plain hated his old man, the bossing around, the strict discipline, the constant need to live up to him and never pleasing him?

And was that the reason he was now here? He wanted to please no one but himself now, and that meant disagreeing with Sydney.

Colorado, or at least this part of it, was greener and more fertile than the Wyoming he knew. But as he set off into the Rockies, he realized it wasn't any less dangerous. It was a very narrow trail through the chasms leading into Estes Park—a trail on which anyone could be hiding above, take a pot-shot at him, corner him. The peaks only conjured up protection, towering above, their pinnacles skewering the sky and hiding the sun. The clouds sitting above had an outline glow as the sun set low behind them, but in the morning as he set off, the sky was spread out in colors like lantern oil on water, diffused. The snow on the peaks was blue in the morning light.

All too beautiful to be thinking of killing.

****

When Sydney missed her menses the first month, she wasn't alarmed. She knew upset and fatigue could have such an effect. She hadn't as yet left the town because she believed she was of help here, people now appreciated her, and if Shiloh returned it didn't mean she would let him back in her bed or marry him. She was her own woman now, independent of the men who had tried to rule her life—her father and Garnforth most notably. And if she did leave, where would she go? Could she just pick herself up and start over somewhere else? And wouldn't Shiloh find her if he wanted, if he returned?

But while her patients now included women, especially those expecting an addition to their family, few spoke to her on a social level and none invited her to dine at their homes. The evenings were lonely; she hadn't crossed the divide into being socially acceptable as a single female doctor, and her attendance on the doves at the The Painted Lady certainly did not help, nor was it something she felt she could give up.

On a Sunday after church, with the usual small talk in the front yard and pleasantries that went nowhere, she changed hurriedly after a small bite to eat at home and saddled up her newly purchased mare to go visit

Bones.

She found him sitting on the front porch, whittling and humming to himself, and he graced her with the biggest smile she'd seen in a very long time.

"Well, lookee here! Doctor Cantrell! Well, I'll be damned."

"Hopefully not, Bones." She slid down from her horse and tied her to the rail out front of the homestead. "Though from the way folks in town act, you'd think association with me would certainly damn people to hell."

Bones let out a throaty laugh. "You expected that, I believe. Well, there ain't no changin' some folks, I'm afraid. But I sure is glad to see you. You come on in, let me fix you something."

"That's very kind, but just tea will do nicely if you still have some."

"I sure do." He stood and put his whittling knife and a horse figure aside before preceding her into the house.

He studied her as he got the two mugs down from a shelf and found the tea leaves. He pumped some water into the kettle and set it on the range. "You lookin' real healthy now. I bet that trip back east helped clear your head a bit and you're real happy to be back here now."

"I am happy to be back here, Bones. I'm glad the Indians at the reservation have someone to look after them they're maybe more comfortable with, and I'm certainly thankful for the lovely office and home Shiloh built me."

"You go up to the fort any?"

"No. I think if the laundresses up there need me, they'll come to town. There's plenty to keep me busy in town now, so I'm afraid I've had to make that decision. There's no love lost between me and the colonel, I'm sure."

The kettle whistled, and Bones lifted it to pour the boiled water into the two mugs with leaves. "I'm afraid we ain't got no teapot, but if you don't drink right to the bottom you should be fine. I guess you remember that." He passed over her mug as she pulled a chair from the table and eased into it.

"I'm sure it'll be fine. Just being here makes things fine."

He glanced across at her, a sterner look on his deep brown face. "You feel that way, you should be lettin' Mr. Shiloh know that."

The mug was halfway to her mouth when she responded, "I have let Shiloh know that, Bones. Shiloh knows exactly how I feel. About everything." She sipped, Bones' stare making her feel uncomfortable. "Do you think I should leave the house now, since I've terminated my relationship with him?"

"Terminated?"

"Ended."

Bones shook his head. "You done that? Why'd you go ahead and do that, Doc? That man is crazy 'bout you."

She tucked a strand of hair behind an ear. How would Bones have known about her relationship with Shiloh? Shiloh had left after their contretemps. And was it any of Bones' business? She supposed it was, in a way, and it was certainly good to have someone to talk to, even if he was most likely partial to Shiloh rather than herself.

"I...I cannot condone his killing. I've told him that

numerous times."

Bones leant back against the counter of the kitchen worktable and stared up at the ceiling as if answers to whatever he was thinking were written there. After a moment, he pulled out a chair, placed his mug on the table, and sat, scrutinizing Sydney as if she, too, had something written on her face. "He gone after the man what killed his sister, tried to kill you too, I believe."

"He had something to do with it, that man, but I'm not sure he was there that night."

"And you don't approve?" He sat back in the chair as she sipped her tea, meeting his gaze over the top of her mug.

"I think he should have left this to the law, let the sheriff or a marshal get this man. It's not Shiloh's place, it's not his job, it's ”

"Maybe not his job, but he feel guilt for not bein' here to protect his sister. He sees it as his job now."

She sighed. "I think you know what I'm saying, Bones. He should have left it to someone else."

"You worried 'bout Mr. Shiloh gettin' killed?"

"Of course." She dragged out the words as if the thought hurt her so much she couldn't continue. "But I also have a moral objection to his going in and killing this man in retribution."

"But you ain't got no moral 'jection to someone else killing this man, if need be. You know Mr. Shiloh prefer to take the man alive if he can, but they never gives in. Never. Every one think they's the smartest, they's the best. They gonna fight to the bitter end, Doc. They always do. And it ain't Mr. Shiloh's fault. Never. I seen it with my own eyes. And it's like the meat on your plate: you have no 'jection to someone else killing that steer, but you sure's not goin' to kill it yo'self."

Sydney sat thinking for a long time, sipping her tea, snatching glances at Bones as he continued to stare at her and drink from his own mug. At last she said in a voice so low the old man had to lean forward to hear, "I can't help myself, Bones. It's the way I feel. I do love him, and I know he loves me. But I just can't bear the thought of his killing, of going after this man with the intention, the desire, to murder him. That's all."

****

Despite Shiloh's care, Whiskey had thrown a shoe on the rocky road down through the mountain canyons and along the Big Thompson River. There were cabins dotted along the river, but Shiloh didn't stop for help or want to ask for shelter at any of these. They could be fishermen's or hunters' cabins, or they could be outlaws' shacks, it was debatable, and he had no plan to end up with his provisions and his horse and mule gone and himself dead. He would find out Yeager's whereabouts sure enough in Estes Park.

He'd heard once the land was owned by some English lord or other, Dunraven, but of late the Englishman had pretty much left and local ranchers and others were moving in against this lord's claims. There was a village of sorts now, around the lake. He'd camp there for the night, find a blacksmith or farrier in the morning, and start asking questions. Try to find this Claudine, the French whore.

As he made camp under an untold number of stars, he thought again of Sydney, of her beauty, her goodness, but also her stubbornness in not seeing his way. He'd have to teach her, sometime, compromise was a good thing; he had accepted her leaving for

Philadelphia knowing dang well she would come back. Now she had to adjust to his ways, his desire to avenge his sister's death and find the man that had also had a lot to do with the attack on her. Surely, she could understand all that.

Morning came with the soft light of stars fading, sun gently giving its brilliance to the earth below, birdsong filling the air, the dew of morning mist settling on flowers and grasses giving off a perfume that could never be captured, sparkling, and the moist air that had not as yet burnt off. He lay in his bedroll for several moments before stretching out to get his muscles going after the hard night.

A twig snapped. The Colts were in his hands and he was on his belly when a shout came: "Hello the camp!"

"You come in easy, hands raised." Shiloh scooted back on his knees and dropped one Colt where he could get it, keeping his gaze in the direction of the shout.

The man stepped into the clearing, leading a chestnut mare laden with bedroll and rifle. One eye was half closed with a scar running through, bushy dark eyebrows giving him a mean, ornery look.

"Well, Aiden Jeffers." Shiloh lowered his gun. "If it ain't the devil himself."

"Shiloh Coltrane, as I live and breathe. Would hardly recognize you with that beard." Jeffers lowered his hands and extended one, which Shiloh shook. "Let me guess—Yancy Yeager?"

"Have a cup of coffee, Jeff. Find yourself a seat."

Shiloh sifted the ashes and got the fire going again before he started making coffee, shuffling around as he listened to Jeffers loosening the cinch on his horse and doing his own chores. When Shiloh had settled, and the fire was back up, he stared across at Jeffers, certain the same question was pretty much on each mind. "You going after Yeager as well?"

"I am. And I hadn't planned on splitting the bounty."

"I'm not interested in the bounty, Jeff; it's all yours. I'm just interested in Yeager being dead."

"That's unusual. Not that you ever were a bounty hunter, as I recollect, but what's your interest in Yeager?"

"Twofold. One, he killed my sister and nephew. Two, he was mostly responsible for almost killing my betrothed."

"Your betrothed!" Jeffers guffawed and sat back, a wide smile almost making him approachable. "I never figured you for the marrying kind."

"Yeah, well. Times change."

"So they do, so they do." He kept his one good eye focused on Shiloh as he poured the coffee into two tin cups and handed one across to Jeffers. "Well, you were pretty much a man of his word, as I recall. That still true?"

"It is—the bounty's yours. I have no interest in blood money now. Fact is, I wanted out of the game until I returned home to find my kin dead. Guess the cards I was dealt made a slightly different hand to what I reckoned on." He took a swig of the coffee and gazed into the pool of black. "I just want to get back in one piece and get married is all. But I want to see Yeager dead first."

"Guess you got as good a reason as any." Jeffers gulped down his coffee and handed the cup over to

Shiloh. "Two men working together is a much better bet than one alone, or two separately. We've worked together before. I say we join forces. What do you say, Coltrane?"

"Suits me." Shiloh threw the dregs of coffee away and wiped out the pot and cups. He shuffled in his bag for some jerky and offered it over to the other man, but Jeffers shook his head.

"There's a café in town, about an hour's ride in. Bacon and eggs would suit me better."

"Yeah, I could eat proper grub." He started to get his things tidied. "Tell me one thing, Jeffers."

"What's that?"

"You got any idea where Yeager is?"

Jeffers gave what passed for a laugh but was more of a snort that ended with his coughing. "'Course I do. You mean to tell me you don't have any idea?"

"I know Estes Park is where he's hanging out, apparently with some French whore, but exactly where, no, I don't know. I figured I'd spend some time in town finding out."

"You ever been into the Rockies this way? Through them parks and all?"

"Nope." Shiloh wondered whether he'd been a fool to try to find Yeager on his own in the first place, but all he'd been able to think about was getting his man and getting home.

"Well, I'd say it was a damn good thing I found ya, then. After Estes Park, the trail thins out into the mountains, following a ridge that eventually leads down to a place, Steamboat Springs—there's the beginning of a town there now. Yeager, from what I understand, but can't of course confirm, hides out in a shack somewhere along that ridge. Difficult to get to if you don't know the trail, and impossible in winter."

Shiloh thought back to his original plan to come after Yeager last winter and realized what a fool idea that had been. The sheriff had been right. He'd never been much of a tracker, it was true, but he knew he had a way of getting his man.

Jeffers stood. "Well. I'm for bacon and eggs. Sets a man up right well for a killing."

Shiloh liked Jeffers. He'd been pleasant company on the hire they'd both done, protecting a Wyoming rancher from the supposed rustlers just before the invasion during the Johnson County War. It was Shiloh's first hire, and he'd been so young they almost didn't take him on. There'd been a lot of battles during that Wyoming range war, and both men had luckily stayed on the same side.

As they rode along there was a companionable quiet; Jeffers wasn't a big talker, which Shiloh also liked, and he was good with a gun, a clear thinker, and calm with it.

"Got married since I last saw you."

Shiloh was pulled from his reveries. He gazed across at Jeffers, a sting of jealousy hitting him hard. "No kidding. Congratulations." He reached a hand across to shake the other man's with good wishes.

"Never thought a woman would take to an old bandit like me, one good eye and all, but she's as fine a woman as ever lived. And got two kids with her as well."

"Well, I'll be." Shiloh ran a hand through the straggly growth on his face. He wasn't quite used to it as yet but couldn't be bothered to shave, either. That would come in time. "Where they living?"

"Utah. Mormon. Not me, of course, but the community is welcoming. Sort of. Try to convert me regularly, but I skedaddle too often to take to it, and I'm in the wrong line of business, of course."

Shiloh laughed. "Guess it suits you."

"It's great. Really. Love her like the dickens. You'll find out, wait you see."

****

When she missed the second month and began to feel queasy in the mornings, Sydney knew the die was cast. There was no way back, and the way forward was fraught with obstacles. If she hadn't been popular in town before, her condition would mark her with the proverbial scarlet letter for sure; having a child out of wedlock would just prove the point, confirm what all the proper ladies of the town thought all along about a woman doctor.

There was no word nor sign from Shiloh. She had visited Bones several times; it had pretty much become a regular Sunday outing for her after church, to go up there and call on him, see how he was doing on his own. Occasionally she had met a man named Bates, a smallholder from a neighboring parcel who helped out once in a while and, in return, Bones apparently helped him. But there was no word from Shiloh, no notice of his whereabouts, whether he was alive or dead or shot up somewhere. And even if he returned, Sydney had told him she wouldn't marry him, and she felt she must stick to her decision, to her conscience.

There was no doubt that sometimes at night she absolutely longed for him to be there next to her, feel his touch, experience his kiss, his love. And she knew for certain he would make a loving, caring father. But there was still that thought in the back of her mind, that fear—one day he would pick up his guns once more and go after someone as he was going after Yeager now. Or someone would come looking for him—in retribution. She couldn't face it.

A plan was necessary.

She knew she would be showing by the fourth month; up until then the loose coat she wore as a doctor would cover any telltale signs, the slight thickening around her waist. Then she would have to leave. Before then, the first thing she had to do was wire the medical school and ask to advertise for a recent graduate who would come to assist.

And then, in time, he or she would take over.

Chapter Seventeen

Questioning folk in Estes Park brought up no knowledge of a Claudine or a French whore of any kind. Both men thought the locals were tight-lipped, perhaps afraid of Yeager. The next step was to search for what Jeffers believed to be the outlaw's hideout—a shack on the trail to Steamboat Springs. It was a strenuous three days down the trail the bounty hunter had described. Shiloh was glad he had brought the pack mule instead of a second horse. The horses could just about deal with the steep, rocky road, but the mule, laden with provisions, didn't give him any trouble and led the horses on.

He and Jeffers got to know each other better, became reacquainted. He liked the man, felt he was trustworthy and a good companion, and hoped Jeffers felt the same regarding him.

"You know if Yeager has any men with him? You don't know how many there might be?"

"No idea." Jeffers leant well back in his saddle as they traveled a steep peak downhill, snaked back and forth as the trail descended, bowing under branches and holding them aside. It was slow going.

"I like to know about how many men I'm up against." He put his hand up to push a branch out of the way and moved his horse and mule aside for Jeffers to pass.

"As do I," the older man asserted. "But these outlaw hideouts, as you no doubt know, they can be empty with all of 'em gone or they can have a load of men sitting around and waiting to outsmart the law. No telling."

Shiloh swore under his breath. "No telling is no plan."

"Nope. I'm afraid it's wait and see."

"But I think we're at a place we might be wise now to get off the trail and cover our tracks. If anyone has spotted us, they may just think we're on the way to Steamboat, or they may decide we're after the bounty and mean harm. And I know which I'd be prepared for if I was one of them." He pushed his hat back and took an appraisal of the lay of the land.

"Getting off the trail looks pretty dangerous. What do you suggest?" Jeffers glanced down the mountain, its cover of rock and brush and tall trees.

"Well, that's why I haven't mentioned it 'til now. But I think we've gone far enough to start worrying." He pulled up. "Let's make camp, then. There's some thick brush over yonder. No fire. We should have good cover. Maybe I'll go on for a bit, on foot, see what's what. Do you think it's far?"

"No. I'm pretty certain it can only be a mile or so on. That's why I say if we get off the trail now, let's circle round in the morning."

Shiloh dismounted and led Whiskey to the area where the brush would cover them from any riders on the track. He started to pull some of his equipment from the mule to bed down for the night before he went on to see if he could find the cabin.

"I'll do that if you want to go," Jeffers offered.

"Just come back in one piece."

He swapped his Colts for the Smith and Wessons he had brought and slung one of the Winchesters over his shoulder on its strap. He checked the magazine was full before setting off, slipping and sliding downhill and trying to scratch out his path every so often as he went. He figured it was about an hour and a half or more before he spotted a cabin, low and hardly visible, set into the hillside with a small corral to its side. A thin string of smoke reached for the sky. Two horses.

Shiloh sat back behind a stand of pine. He raised the rifle, testing the distance in his mind, and waited a while to see if anyone came out. There was a lantern in the window, and beyond he could make out one form moving about inside. A second man eventually came out to get some feed to the horses in the corral.

Two.

A tiny finger of fear made him shiver for a moment. Yeager had never been taken down, and many men had tried. Shiloh had been in many situations where he'd proved his nerves of steel, but never before had he had a woman he loved so much as he loved Sydney, a woman he wanted to return to, have a home with, kids. He had to do this, *he had to*, and he had to succeed. But there was no point in starting this on his own. He'd go back to Jeffers, and the two would work together. Tomorrow? Or tonight?

When he got back to camp, his old friend had it laid out and a small fire for coffee going. Shiloh swallowed his annoyance; after all, he may have said, "No fire," but he wasn't the boss or leader—they were working together.

Jeffers sat up. "Had to make a fire," he explained

before being asked. "No fire, no coffee."

Shiloh stooped down and took the proffered mug. "Doesn't matter now. I think we have to act. Tonight. There's a cabin a ways down, and I spotted only two men there, and two horses. If we wait 'til morning, there may be more coming in."

"Did you see Yeager?"

"Can't tell who the hell is there 'cept, as I said, it's two—two horses, two men."

The older man thought a moment, his head bowed, peering into the fire. "I'm not out to kill just anyone, Coltrane."

"I know that. Neither am I. But we can't exactly knock and ask if Yeager is at home. Here's what I suggest..."

****

Dark came as it often does in the mountains, a split-second break from daylight with a chill of clear, dry air. The moon was a silver sliver, often hiding behind fast-moving clouds. The two men got within sight of the cabin together, then split sides, Shiloh going to the front where he had seen the lantern in the window. He sat back, re-checking the magazine in the Winchester—five shots, fully loaded. And he watched as Jeffers practically crawled into the corral, silent as a cat, and led the two horses out and into the trees before shooing them off.

When he mimicked an owl's hoot twice, Shiloh got the rifle to his shoulder, levered the cartridge into the chamber, and fired.

The shot went through the paper of the window, shattering the lantern in an explosion of glass that scattered, toppled the base, and lit a wood table. One man escaped through the back, either a door or window, he didn't know. He could hear the report of Jeffers' 1873, followed by loud moaning carried on the wind. That same wind was fanning the fire, which now had caught within the house. Shiloh waited for the second man to appear.

And then he heard the click behind him.

Swiveling, he swung and battered the rifle into the legs of his assailant, knocking him off balance and giving Shiloh time to pull his sidearm. He stood, the revolver in his hand, looking down into the face of a man he remembered but couldn't place. Balsam, that was his name. Wanted for a train robbery a few years back.

Balsam was down, winded, but recovering enough to crawl his hand out in the dirt and reach the Colt he had dropped in the melee. Shiloh fired right into the man's hand, causing him to shout in pain, but he still tried to pull his left gun. One more shot took care of that.

Jeffers was making his way back to the corral, but the flames were now licking out the rear of the cabin. He had reached the man he'd shot and dragged him from danger when a third man came running out front.

Shiloh lifted his rifle, pulled the lever, and fired. And he prayed that was Yancy Yeager.

****

"Balsam gang." Aiden Jeffers squatted over the one dead body before moving on to the man he'd pulled away from the fire. "Damn Yeager. Where is he?"

Shiloh figured that man wouldn't last long enough to get into Steamboat, and he was bandaging the now-tied-up Balsam's two hands, but that outlaw wasn't saying anything either.

"You let me go, I'll let you know where Yeager is." His voice was phlegmy, low.

"No deal. I'll find Yeager and see you hang." Shiloh ran a hand across his face, tempted to scratch his beard. "You tell me where Yeager is, maybe the sheriff will give you life in the penitentiary or something rather than a necktie party."

"Like hell." He spat.

"What's this dying man's name? We ought to know so we can tell his kin."

"Schenk."

"What?"

"Schenk. That's his name. You hard of hearing?"

Shiloh shook his head and strolled over to where Jeffers had tried to make the dying outlaw comfortable in his final hour. He crouched next to the man, noted the burns and blood, and shook his head once more. This was a dirty business, and he wished he hadn't started out on it, but now he was here he couldn't just walk out on his friend.

The dying man was making gurgling sounds as if gasping for air, but his eyes took in Shiloh and gaped at him.

"You're going to meet your maker, I'm afraid." Shiloh could envisage Sydney taking the man's burnt hand in comfort, but it wasn't in his nature. "He might take more kindly to you if you help us out."

"Don't do it, Schenk!" Balsam shuffled around where they had tied him. "You may live. It's a trick!"

Shiloh scrunched his face in distaste.

"If he lives," Jeffers interjected, "It'll go better for him if he helps us out."

"Just tell us," Shiloh continued, "if you know where Yancy Yeager is."

There was the merest nod, the dying man's eyes sinking under closing lids. He mumbled something Shiloh couldn't understand.

"Say again." He bent low over the man, the stench of his breath and body almost making him draw back.

"Brown's Park...Brown's Hole. Yeager...there."

****

"You'd have to be stark raving mad to go to Brown's Hole," the sheriff of Steamboat Springs told the two men. "It's not worth it. You can be weaving about for days...no, months...without finding anyone. It's a maze, that place. Hideouts scattered about, trails leading nowhere, canyons all over the place you'll find nigh on impossible to work. Your horses won't last. Listen to me. Leave Yeager for now. Go back to your wives and live long and happy lives. That bounty is not worth it." He glanced from Shiloh to Jeffers and back, obviously trying to ascertain whether his words had any effect.

Shiloh tilted a questioning glance to Jeffers, who shrugged.

"I need the bounty. I'm counting on it," Jeffers affirmed. "Four thousand! We can but try."

"And speaking of a bounty, there's one on Balsam and his men, nowhere near as much as on Yeager, of course, but it may dissuade you at least from this foolhardiness." The sheriff went to his cash drawer and counted out the sum. "Listen to me, will ya?" He held out the comparatively small sum.

"You take it," Shiloh said. "I just want to see Yeager dead."

201

Jeffers pocketed the money as the sheriff shook his head.

"It's more than a hundred fifty miles, easiest route, just to get to the park. Then you gotta find the bastard. That's at least a five-day ride before you start dealing with the canyons and cliffs."

"We got a pack mule and can take the three horses of the outlaws."

"Son, you're gonna need a helluva lot more than a spare horse or two for that place."

The two men strolled out into the road, exchanged glances.

"We better stock up, I guess."

"You got enough cartridges for those fancy guns of yours?"

"I reckon. I stopped in Cheyenne and loaded up."

"Good. Then promise me one thing, will you?"

"What's that?"

"Anything happens to me, you take the bounty on down to 'Tilda so she has something to feed the kids and start again. She's down in Provo. Works when she can at the woolen mill there; they'll know where to find her."

Shiloh stared long and hard into Aiden Jeffers' eyes. He was glad the man was with him, but he could do this alone if need be. "You sure you wanna come?"

"Like I said, I need the bounty. It's what I'm counting on."

"Let's go get him, then."

They took two spare horses off the three men they'd handed in, the mule packed with fresh provisions. At times Shiloh wondered whether he'd ever see Sydney again, a feeling amplified by Jeffers' questioning as the older man began to feel more and more at ease with his young friend.

"So tell me about this fiancée of yours. What's she like?"

"Doctor. I thought I'd told you."

"Doctor! Well, hell's bells, boy, what kinda woman becomes a doctor?"

"A beautiful, kind, caring one." He couldn't hide his annoyance. "What difference does it make if a woman becomes a doctor? I don't understand the whole hullaballoo. She can study and learn same as a man, can't she?"

"Yeah, but shouldn't she be at home minding little ones? Whatcha gonna do when the babies start coming?"

"We haven't discussed it yet." Shiloh sniffed his disapproval of the cross-examination. "Guess she can look after patients at the same time."

"Well. Guess she can if you want her to." Jeffers avoided continuing the subject now. "I'm happy for you."

"Thanks." He rubbed his forehead and pushed his hat back. *If only Sydney was happy for us too!*

It was a hard five days' ride to the edge of the area known as Brown's Park or Brown's Hole. They wound through hills of sagebrush punctuated by open desert expanses dotted with hard rock gradients, and then whitewater canyons forcing them to wind their way around to find crossings. It was a maze, a nightmare, as the sheriff had said. The only saving grace was the plentiful wildlife that kept them well fed—antelope, deer, moose, and elk, as well as game birds, appeared like they wanted to be eaten. The Green River was the main water feed, cracking the earth as if it had been shattered, and flowing out into smaller canyons in all directions, sculpting mountains and desert into one jagged and coarse landscape.

Shiloh felt they'd come to a place so remote he had fallen off the Earth, yet the climate was mild to begin with, and water, once they got in to the center, plentiful. Onward, they passed sandstone cliffs with hidden caves, rode confusing trails that seemed to switch back onto themselves, and found abandoned cabins they wasted time watching only to discover no one showed up during the time they were there. As the sheriff had said, it was indeed impenetrable. This was part of the so-called Outlaw's Trail, and only the outlaws, it seemed, knew how to navigate this no-man's land. At times, Shiloh even wondered if they'd ever find their way out.

Weeks went by, heat filling the canyons with an intensity Shiloh had never known, sweat drying on his skin before it had time to soak his shirt. They spent time bathing in rivers to cool down, only to get out and be soaked once more by torrential rains that quickly filled the gulches and coulees, crashing through with an explosive sound, stones being carried by the rushing water. As the summer rolled on, the days of searching became a routine of late afternoon thunderstorms, the heat building up until sheet lightning flickered its warning, to be followed by forks of lightning as if the devil himself were throwing his spear. The thunder reverberated around the canyon walls, echoed back at itself until the rain poured down, clearing the air, and calm would be restored, only for the whole process to be repeated next day.

Shiloh often thought of the ranch he'd left behind, of Bones' age and whether he was managing, even if he were still alive, and, most of all, he thought about Sydney. He longed to see her again, try to make amends for his time away, try to get her to understand why he had done this thing, this search for Yeager, and try to get her to accept him as he was. Was she even still there? Had she moved on, gone back east? What had become of the home and office in town he had built? In the years he had been away from home, he had never considered any of this, since his sister and Parmeter were supposedly looking after the ranch; Meg had been the one to inherit it, although he now knew it had been entailed on them both. Now it was his, and his feelings of responsibility were torn between the ranch and this quest on which he had set himself. And Sydney of course, always Sydney, and whether he would ever see her again.

As September rolled in and the days shortened, the men found the heat would sit possessively in the canyons, then relent and leave with a sudden chill. The nights were definitely getting cooler, and both knew soon enough snow could come with the unpredictability the high plains promised.

"We two dang fools or what?" Jeffers poked a branch into the campfire and watched as sparks flew like fireflies on the wind. "I'm thinking maybe we're wandering like those people in the Bible, never getting anywhere. Might be it's time to give in."

Shiloh stayed silent for several moments, thinking it through. "Sort of makes all the last five months worthless, then, don't it? You want to go back to 'Tilda empty-handed?"

Andrea Downing

"I want to go back to 'Tilda is all. I'm thinking she'd rather have me back than not have me at all. What about your woman?"

"Probably gone." The succinctness in his tone held Jeffers from speaking. Shiloh sat back and threw a twig on the fire. "I was never really engaged, Jeff. Was wishful thinking on my part. Love her with everything I got, but I guess we were never meant to be. She couldn't abide my killing, what with her saving lives and all. Never understood why I wanted to get Yeager so bad, how him killing my sister meant I had to take my revenge."

"But you don't know that, do you? That she's gone?"

"'Course not! How the hell would I know whether she's still there or not? I got some special power or something?"

"All right, all right, don't go blowing up at me. I was just asking." Jeffers heaved a sigh. "So, whatcha wanna do, Coltrane? Go on or go back? I'm thinking I may head off, but I'm reluctant to leave you to do this thing alone, now we been together some five months or so. Well, hell, I even lost track of the days."

"October twentieth. I've been counting." He gazed into the fire as if he were reading the writing on the wall. "I built her that office and did every dang thing I knew how to win her over."

"And why'd you lie to me? Telling me you were gonna be wed and all? What was the purpose of that?"

Shiloh looked up, the flames warming his face and dancing shadows as smoke rose. "Wishful thinking. I thought if I said it, it might make it so. She left for a while and I kept telling everyone she was coming back,

206

built the house for her, and just like that, she did return. So I thought if I kept saying it, it would be true."

Jeffers laughed. "Well I'll be. You're a right old fortune teller, ain't ya?"

He laughed at himself. "I guess time will tell, Jeff, time will tell." He sat in a comfortable silence with his friend as the minutes passed, then glanced up.

Jeffers looked solemn now, as if he had reached a decision.

"You want to go, don't you? I think you ought to, you know, before the kids forget who you are."

The older man turned away and flicked out his bedroll. "I'll be off in the morning, then, Coltrane. I've got the money the sheriff gave us for the Balsam gang, and that'll keep us for a while, plus her wages, such as they are, from the mill. We'll get along. You keep the horses, that's all right with me."

"One spare will do me, Jeff, with my mule. You may need the other if trouble comes. They're pretty worn out."

"And so am I," he said, fixing his saddle into place as a pillow. "And so am I."

****

Shiloh woke to find Aiden Jeffers gone, along with one of the two outlaw horses, as agreed. He understood the silent departure; good-byes were not easy in their world, though he hoped one day he might see the man again, meet the wife and kids, although he knew it unlikely. Jeffers had left him most of the provisions, taking only a spare amount of flour and sugar and coffee, probably thinking he'd be to a town soon enough. It was when Shiloh started the fire going for his coffee that he heard the first shot, followed straightaway by a second, which ricocheted around the canyon walls, echoing for several moments as he quickly got his guns together and slung one rifle over his shoulder. The question was, were they shots for help from Jeffers or his death knell?

The horses pranced uneasily at the sounds, light just beginning to show above the canyon walls, blues and pinks coloring a sky that foretold another warm day. He scrutinized the surroundings, studying each cleft in every wall as much as he could, but he saw nothing. The sound had come from the north, he figured, though it was difficult to tell within the granite walls. He fixed the bridle on Whiskey, mounting him bareback, and rode out, keeping close to the bulwarks nature had provided. He kept his gaze roaming, searching all around for any shooter that might be above, beyond, or right in his way.

The only person he spotted was Jeffers. Dead on the trail. His horse grazed nearby and the other with it.

A blinding anger rode through Shiloh, burning his insides, making him tremble with such fury he hardly knew what he was doing. Slipping down, he peered at the rock face above, searched for the shooter, but none was to be found. Yeager. It had to be Yeager. He'd be the only one to shoot without question, leave a dying man there for the hot sun.

"Yeager, you bastard!" he shouted, the words echoing back at him, reverberating off the canyon walls, "I'm coming to get you, Yeager, I'm coming to get you!"

Scanning the horizon and every cleft and ridge, Shiloh had to decide the shooter was gone. From the angle of the shots into Jeffers' chest, it would seem the gunman had been above on one of the high crests and had disappeared now, having left the body to rot and be eaten. The vultures were beginning to circle. Heat wavered the view above. Shiloh cleared Jeffers' pockets of the bounty they had earned, hoping he would get it one day to the wife down in Provo along with his guns and any other personal items he might be able to take to her. The question was what to do now. No shovel to dig a grave. A cairn was one option, but it would be better to somehow get the man into a place the animals couldn't reach. His gaze scanned the hills of granite surrounding the canyon and found one possibility. That would have to do—slide Jeffers into the crevice and close it with a barricade of rocks and stones, scratch a name and cross into the boulder with his knife.

After that, it seemed it would be a matter of time before he found Yeager or Yeager found him.

****

It was a week later, as hail pounded him while he tried to cook up some elk, the first shot pinged off the fry pan. Startled, Shiloh wasn't sure, to begin with, if that was hail ringing on the metal or a bullet, but he grabbed his rifle and scurried for cover. The horses were tied across the clearing in the trees, and he prayed the shooter wouldn't get them, a certain death out here in such wilderness. There was silence for a time, only the sound of the hail hitting ground and bouncing up, the horses restless and dancing in their place, but nothing of the shooter. Unsure he had heard right, Shiloh poked his hat up on a branch from behind the tree and, sure enough, another shot rang out. Above, the gunman was in a good position to take him down, sit it out, unless Shiloh could circle around through the brush

209

cover. That begged the question as to how many there were, a question he could not answer, though he was figuring only one, as more would certainly have fired at the same time.

With the outlaw above, this could be a waiting game, a game he didn't wish to play—especially if it lasted 'til sundown. He started a slow crawl toward the horses, careful not to ruffle any branches, belly down and hat in hand to get around. The silence from the gunman made him nervous, wondered what he was up to.

He soon found out.

The click of a hammer came in the same second Yeager drawled, "You looking for me, Coltrane? I heared tell from about everyone 'tween here and Laramie you got it in for me."

Caught like an animal on all fours, Shiloh knew he couldn't get his hand back for his gun. He peered up into the face of Yancy Yeager, then eased himself back on his knees. "You gonna shoot me, Yeager, you best be getting on with it."

"Well, I think I might jus' do that. Makes no never mind to me why you been after me."

"You killed my sister…"

Hatred made him strong. He had Yeager's attention, the other thinking he had the upper hand. In a flash, Shiloh grabbed Yeager's leg, forcing the outlaw off balance so that he tumbled as his gun fired, the shot taking down a branch. Shiloh was on top of him, struggled to get the gun loose from his hand as another shot fired and Yeager bit his arm, throwing Shiloh over on his back. As the gunman tried to get to his feet, Shiloh pulled his own leg up to knee Yeager in the groin. Yeager doubled in pain. Shiloh got his knife from his boot, pushing it up deep into Yeager's gut, the gun falling from his hand. As Yeager collapsed, Shiloh scrambled to stand over his adversary, easing his own gun from his holster and pointing it into the outlaw's face.

"Do it already," the killer said. "Don't leave me here for the vultures."

Shiloh knelt down. "Like you left Jeffers? I'd love to see you picked to death. They start on the eyes first, don't they? Or eaten by coyotes and wolves, a right picnic for them. I'd love to see you bake in the heat here, starve to death as you died, but me, I'm in a hurry to get home now, get your damned body to Steamboat and collect the bounty, get that money to Jeffers' widow way over in Provo, and head for home up in Wyoming. So I'm going to be real kind to you, Yeager. Real kind."

And with that, he shot Yancy Yeager through the heart.

Chapter Eighteen

Sydney lay in Shiloh's bed at the ranch, the baby sucking contentedly, a sheet pulled up for modesty as Bones looked on.

"Well, I never thought I'd be playing midwife. That's a new one on this old man. Thought we'd be able to get out your lady doctor friend. Lord had diff'rent idees, it seems."

Sydney pushed a strand of damp hair from her face and peered down at her daughter. Shiloh's daughter. "I sort of thought so, too, Bones, but you did an excellent job. Really."

"I'd say I had an excellent teacher. You instructin' and pushin' at the same time and all. Shall I head to town now for the other doc?"

"No, Evelyn will be dealing with patients, as she has for the last five months since I've been up here." She laid her head back on the pillow and switched the newborn to her other side. "I must say having another woman sent by the college was a stroke of luck. I felt more comfortable confiding in her than if they'd sent a man. And maybe this way the town will see a woman doctor is what they're getting—one of us anyway, if not both. A male doctor might have been such a hit he'd have left me without a job to return to."

"You think you'll go back?"

"I don't know. I need time with my daughter, time

to think things out. It's obvious, after all these months, Shiloh won't be returning." She pushed down the emptiness inside her, as she had been doing ever since he had left. "What will you do, Bones?"

He sat on a chair in the corner and glanced across at the pair in bed. "I ain't got no place else to be, so I'll just go on as I have been. Some folks not too keen on a colored man having the ranch, but Boss did leave papers leaving it all to me, with an income to you. I never did file them, of course, but if it comes to it, I will. You need money?"

"I don't think so—Evelyn gives me a cut of what she makes, as I think I told you, since it's technically my office. In time, I may be able to go back to work. We'll see."

"Whatcha gonna name that sweet child?"

Sydney glanced down at her beautiful baby. "Margaret. For Shiloh's sister. It'd be only right, and what he'd want, I'm sure."

Bones shook his head in agreement. "Maybe you forgive him now? For going after Yeager?"

"I don't know. I keep thinking if he hadn't gone maybe we would've worked things out, had a life together eventually. But he did go, left me—us—and now I find it even harder to think kindly on him. I can't mourn him; it's been too long not knowing. But I miss him still." She peered down again at the sleeping child in her arms. "Then again, I think maybe I've been too harsh, too judgmental. I did, after all, have to kill three men in self defense, so I can't say I'm much different from Shiloh, can I?"

Bones rested an elbow on the dresser by his side, weariness obviously overcoming him. It'd been a long night and day waiting for that baby to come. "You gonna live here? You're welcome to, for sure. It's what Shiloh'd want."

"I know, Bones, but I have enough of a reminder of Shiloh with Margaret here, and I think I have to try to make my way on my own. I could go back to town, but I don't think I'm ready as yet to face the townspeople. And the baby would be crying and making life difficult for Evelyn, who really has enough on her hands."

Bones stood and peered out the window. "Another dang snowstorm. I'm so fed up with these storms, I'd be tempted to head on back to Texas, 'cepting they're none so friendly to the colored as here. Leastways here they're pleasant enough and deal honest with me. Though maybe they're fearing if Shiloh returns he'll give them hell if they don't." He was silent a moment, watching the snow pelt the window and slide down the pane. "You're welcome to stay, but if going's what you're set on, there's an old line camp a way out. It's just a two-room shack, really, with a corral and shed barn, but you can make it homey for a while, 'til you're ready to face the world again. And it ain't so far out as you can't reach me if you need me, or come for a visit. 'Course, you run the same risks as you done at your old cabin." He turned to look on the child again. "I'd sure 'preciate seeing that sweet child time and again."

Sydney eased herself out of bed, the baby in her arms. The pain in her groin and stomach was abating somewhat but still made it difficult to move with any speed. She held the baby close to her but reached a hand out to feel the smooth finish of the cradle Bones had made her. "This is so beautiful, Bones. I still can't get over you making this for us."

"Least I could do. And it give me pleasure to do so."

"I don't think the minister will christen a bastard child, but I'd like it if you'd act as godfather to her. Will you?"

"'Course I will. I surely will, Doc, I surely will. And proud to do so."

****

Sydney leaned her shotgun against the wall by the cabin door and peeked down at the baby once more. She took up a clean rag, certain if she saw one more spider or any more mice droppings she'd just head on back to the ranch and give up this idea of the line camp. Meg, as she called the baby, slept soundly, and if she fussed, all it took was a little rocking in the cradle to send her back to sleep until feeding time came around again. A pail of soaking diapers stood nearby waiting for a wash with lye soap.

When she heard the trundling wagon coming through the clearing, she fetched up the gun and went to the door to make sure it was Bones. Seeing his huge grin, she replaced the shotgun and strode out to meet him.

"Well, you look like the cat that got the cream!"

"Ha! I'm the cat what got the cook stove, and cheap, too." He pulled his brake and hopped down from the wagon seat. "Bates's on his way over to help. Soon's we get this thing set up right and some wood chopped, you be in business with a kitchen. Then I 'spect to be invited over to 'dine' with you." He made a playful bow.

Sydney laughed. "Well, what do I owe you for it?" She peered into the wagon bed, took in the Quaker

Social cook stove, and breathed a deep, happy breath. "Wow, that's something. Where did you get that?"

"Mercantile told me Mrs. Bender selling it. Brought in some newfangled stove from back east, thinks it bigger and better than this, but I tell you Quaker's is the best. We lucky. Don't cost much. Ten dollar, and I put it on account."

She clasped Bones' shoulder. "Oh, Bones, I owe you so much…for everything. I'll pay you back when I can."

"Don't you worry, Doc. Way I see it, it's Shiloh's money and he owe you that much, if not more."

Inside, the baby started mewling once again.

As Sydney turned to go in, Bones said, "I think I'll start chopping the fallen trees out yonder. That way, soon's Bates shows up we can get this thing going."

"Oh, Bones. You're so good to me." She swiped some tears away as she headed for the house.

"Woman needs a man," he called after her.

Yes, and a baby needs a father.

She found she had hours to think, nursing the baby, caring for Meg, making a home for her here. When Bates arrived, the action started and Meg awoke, so Sydney sat in the back room, where her cot was, nursing the child. Always during that time, it came over her Shiloh had died thinking she didn't love him enough to have him return. Maybe he didn't care if he died or not, maybe his one aim was to get that man, Yeager, and that was all he cared about since she had told him she wouldn't have him. It filled her with an emptiness that would remain with her all her days. She knew she would watch Margaret grow, her blonde hair and features just like Shiloh's, and always think of what

216

might have been, how the child's father could have returned to them and they might have been a family with other children coming. So often, to her dying day, she would wonder what had happened to him and whether she had made the right decision. Telling him it was wrong to go after his sister's killer had been the right thing to do, but she knew now she could have done it differently, not been so insistent she wouldn't have him back. Would that have made a difference?

She'd never know.

****

As Shiloh rode into town, the first person he spotted was Sheriff Barnes leaning against a post on the boardwalk outside his office. He realized he was hardly recognizable, long hair hanging out of his Stetson, more than a month of beard since he'd left Widow Jeffers, who'd lent him her dead husband's razor to clean up before he went on. Barnes examined him, no doubt thinking he was trouble, a drifter, until Shiloh pulled up in front of him and sat his horse for a long moment, staring into the sheriff's eyes.

"Well, I'll be… Shiloh Coltrane. Alive and apparently well…sort of, I guess."

"And Yeager dead, Sheriff. Job done."

"Took you long enough. How long you been gone?"

"Coming up to ten months, I reckon." He glanced down the street toward the doctor's office. "Anyway, just thought, as I seen you standing here, I'd let you know."

"Well. Congratulations, then. And I'll say I hope that's the end of the matter, that you're not planning on anything more than a hot bath and a shave."

"First thing I'm planning on is seeing the doc." He started to pull Whiskey away.

"Which one?"

Shiloh stopped where he was. "What d'ya mean, which one?"

"Doc Cantrell more or less disappeared a while back, though word has it she's up at your ranch, Bones looking after her. Doc Evelyn, as she likes to be known, is in the office you built."

"Sydney's living with Bones?" He ran a hand down his face, confusion running through him like a wildfire through dry brush. *Why would she do that?*

"No one's rightly sure. Bones comes in every so often, doesn't say a thing about nothing, and Bates is the only one who's seen her up there, and that's all he'll say. Doc Evelyn doesn't gossip, and no one else goes up to your ranch. So your guess is as good as anyone's, quite honestly."

"Well I guess I'll find out." He spurred his horse and trotted on down the street to the office, dismounting and tying up to a few curious stares.

The door was locked. The sign in the window just said, "The Doctor is out." No use in hanging around to ask questions that might not be answered when he could be making time for the ranch and Sydney, or at least Bones, so he mounted up once more and headed out. The idea of the barbershop bath was left behind.

More than two hours later, his bones aching and tired as all-get-out, he sat on the ridge overlooking his ranch. Minutes from his home, a sob escaped him, surprised him with its suddenness as he swiped away tears. His ordeal was over, a journey he'd never counted on. The weeks searching for Yeager through

Estes Park and Brown's Park finally got to him, but then having to go on back to Steamboat to claim the bounty, make sure the money was wired to Provo, heading down to Provo, recounting the loss of Jeffers to his widow and making himself useful for a few days there, leaving her Jeff's personal stuff and the horses and mule so he could make good time back to his ranch, only to be held up for weeks by several blizzards. And now learning Sydney may have disappeared. Had he made the right decision in going on this quest? Losing Sydney? Thank goodness Bones was still there.

And think of the devil, the old man sauntered out of the house as he watched, started to do his afternoon chores.

As Shiloh spurred his horse down the trail to the house, Bones peered up to see who was coming, tilted his head this way and that, uncertainty written in the lines of his face as the younger man approached.

"You got a bed for me, old man?" he asked in jest as he dismounted.

Bones stood staring, his hands hung at his side. "Wha...wha...what? Is...is that you?"

Shiloh grabbed him in a bear hug. "No one else, old pardner." He held the shaking man at arm's length. "Who'd you think it was?"

"The devil hisself, that's who, with that face like a mountain lion. And where'd the other half of you go? I be the one calling you Bones now."

Shiloh scanned himself. "Am I that bad?"

"Well, you sure's in need of a bath and a haircut, I'll say that."

He gave a brief laugh. "Time enough for that. Where's Sydney? Sheriff said he thought she was living

219

out here. Was she ill? Another doctor in her place and all, was something wrong?" He couldn't keep the fear from his voice.

"Not exactly...*wrong*. You best come on inside. See to that horse of yourn, and I'll get some vittles going for you. You sure looks like you can use 'em."

"I really want to see Sydney first, Bo—"

"You do as I say and then I'll let you go see the doc!"

There was something in his voice that stopped Shiloh in his tracks, and he knew there'd be no arguing with his old friend. Was she married? Ill? The only way to find out seemed to be to do as Bones said. Fear flickered through him, a yearning for her, just to see her, though he knew that wouldn't be enough.

When he finally opened the door to his homestead, the aroma of the old man's cooking hit him, his stomach rumbling with hunger and craving. He hadn't had a decent meal for over two months now, not since 'Tilda Jeffers had fed him and they'd eaten in near silence except for the whine of the kids. But she'd be doing real well now with that bounty on Yeager, and he hadn't felt bad about leaving her to sort her life, maybe buy a place in Provo or Salt Lake and get the kids some decent schooling.

Bones stirred a stewpot, beef and vegetables in a rich gravy, and Shiloh thought maybe he was dreaming.

"Sit down," Bones ordered.

"You gonna tell me where Sydney's gone, or do I have to beat it out of you?"

"You sit and eat, and I'll tell you soon enough." The old man dished up a bowl and grabbed a fork and spoon, then nodded toward the washbasin. "You better be washing your hands afore you sit at my table."

Shiloh laughed. "Your table? You filed those papers, my will, already?"

"'Course not. Why I be doin' that for when you alive?"

"So you didn't give up on me?"

Bones set the bowl and cutlery on the table as Shiloh scrubbed in the basin, a brush and soap getting his hands reasonably clean.

"I didn't know what to think, Boss. But without no proof you's dead, I wasn't making any claims. I jus' keep on working the ranch, Bates too, at times, to help. Winter wasn't bad, and we kept the place runnin'."

"Winter wasn't bad? I got caught in a series of blizzards down in Colorado. Couldn't move out my camp for weeks on end. Half froze to death, half starved to death."

He settled into a chair at the table. Anxious to hear what happened to Sydney, he took in a deep breath before shoveling in his first mouthful. He chewed as if he'd forgotten how.

Bones eased himself down opposite, and his face was creased as if the elderly ranch hand couldn't figure what to say next.

"You gonna tell me where Sydney's gone, then?" He had a spoonful halfway to his mouth.

Bones scrubbed his face with his hand before he cupped his chin, elbow on table.

As Shiloh shoved in his second mouthful, the old man said, "You a pappy."

His coughing and spluttering lasted several minutes as the spoon clattered to the table and he reached for a cloth off the range, wiped his mouth, cleared his throat several times, and finally covered his mouth with his hand, staring hard at Bones.

"Coupla months after you gone, Doc come and tell me. Say she gonna work for another two months, 'til that baby start to show, then she gonna have ta leave. She sent to her old medical school for another doctor to join her, not knowin' of course whether it be a man or a woman doctor, but they done sent her Doc Evelyn. A woman. So she happy. She tell me she gonna leave but she not sure where 'cause unwed mamas not welcome in towns. So I says—"

Shiloh pushed his chair back and stood, towering over Bones. "Where is she now?"

Bones shook his head. "You gonna sit and finish that dang meal I cooked ya, then you wash and shave and clean yo'self up afore I tell you anything."

He took the few steps to stand right next to Bones, threatening as much as he could his old friend. "Damn it, Bones! Tell me where she is!"

Bones turned watery eyes up to him. "You go in that mood, she never take you back. Now you sit and cool some, eat your dinner. You not even ask 'bout the baby!"

Shiloh slumped into his chair, rocked forward and back until he could get a grip on himself. "Boy or girl?"

"Girl. She name her Margaret, Meg, for your sister."

There was a howl of such intensity and pain, Shiloh wasn't even sure it came from him. He pushed the bowl of stew out of the way, Bones reaching out to stop it from falling off the table as Shiloh laid his head down, his body racked by sobs. So much emotion seared through him he couldn't handle it, couldn't think, but he knew if he didn't win Sydney back he wouldn't be able to go on with himself. Not only had he missed the birth of his child, left the only woman he'd ever loved, but she, in turn, had honored his sister, dealt with having a bastard child, got on with her life somehow, without him. His love for her was so intense, it felt like it was burning a hole within him, creating an emptiness that would never be filled unless she would have him back.

When the sobs subsided, he grabbed up the kitchen cloth once more and blew his nose, wiped away the tears and mucus from his face, Bones looking on.

"Tell me where she is, Bones, please God, tell me where she is."

"The line camp shack. We fix it up—"

Shiloh yanked open the door before Bones could finish, but the old man rushed to the door.

"You take Daisy now. Don't you ride that poor horse of yours!"

****

It seemed to be a constant battle with the mice and other creatures—or "varmints" as Bones called them—that made their way into her cabin, but sweeping at least twice a day kept the filth down. Meg was asleep in her cradle, and Sydney thought of sitting out and reading another one of the books that Evelyn had brought up from town. At times she didn't know what she'd have done had the college not sent another female physician; they'd become fast friends, and Evelyn seemed to understand the predicament she had got herself into without judging her—at least not to her face. And then there was Bones, as good a man as any, coming up to check on her at least twice a week and she, in turn, going to visit with him.

The sun was getting lower in the sky, casting an orange glow across the tops of the pine, their scent drifting out on a warm wind. She felt happy and sad all at once, knew that one day she'd have to move on, pretend she was widowed, and try to start again somewhere. But that was a time off and, for now, living here on Shiloh's ranch was a blessing. How stupid had she been to tell him she wouldn't have him? To send him off with those words? She ached to see that funny half-smile of his, the shaggy blond hair and flint eyes that softened when he looked at her, longed for his touch and kiss.

She was deep in these thoughts when she spotted the rider through the trees, stationary, watching, as if he were making a plan. She dashed inside and fetched her shotgun, held it aimed in his direction, ready to shoot if he made a move.

I've killed three men, I can kill one more.

He slowly emerged between two pines and sat, staring across the clearing, the raised gun pointed in his direction.

For a moment, Sydney thought she recognized the horse, one of Bones' mares, but at this distance, she couldn't be sure. She kept the gun aimed on the intruder, ready in case he made a sudden move. Bones had warned her about living out here on her own, same as when she had lived in the cabin that had burnt. He'd told her to stay at the ranch, but she wouldn't listen. Now she wished she had. She fretted if anything happened to her, what would happen to Meg?

"You gonna shoot your baby's pappy?" There was a catch in his voice, as if it took great effort to get the words out.

Sydney lowered the shotgun a few inches, held tight and ready to shoot if he moved any more. She couldn't unravel the words in her mind, they didn't make sense. *Baby's pappy, did he say?*

After a few moments of this standoff, he shouted again, "It's me, Sydney. I've come home. I want to see you, marry you, and I want to see our baby."

Confused, she lowered the gun a little more.

"You're not gonna shoot me, you know that. Put the dang gun down." He let the horse come another foot or so toward the cabin.

Sydney raised the gun to her sight. "Don't you move another inch! I'll shoot, I swear."

"You gonna shoot your baby's father? Ten months I've waited to see you, longed to see you, hold you, love you. I didn't know we had a child, Syd. I mighta come home if I did. But I got Yeager in the end, and it's finished now."

She lowered the gun to rest on its stock, but still tight in her hand. It was him. *It was him.* Flustered, all she could think to say was, "It took you ten months to get him? You expect me to believe that?"

"Believe what you want. You think I woulda stayed away that long if I didn't have to?"

Sydney shook as if trying to rearrange thoughts in her brain. "You stayed away ten months, you can stay away another ten for all I care!"

"You don't mean that, Syd." He let the horse go on another couple of feet. "Leastways let me see our baby. I'm not going 'til I seen her. Bones told me you called her Margaret. You must have some feeling for me if you called her that."

"I did it for your sister, not you, Shiloh. Go away!"

Somewhere inside her she knew she didn't mean it, didn't want him to leave, but she couldn't handle the emotions that flooded their way through her. Part of her didn't want to deal with this reunion, most of her wanted him to get off his dang horse and hold her for an eternity. She wanted to see the hard lines of his face soften when he held Meg, the steel go from his eyes as it did when he made love to her. She just couldn't say it.

"I know you're angry, and I don't know how to make it up to you. But if you let me tell you everything that happened, why it took so long to get home, maybe you'd understand. And I'm not leavin' 'til I see our child."

Inside, the baby was beginning to cry. Sydney stomped from frustration and set the gun to rest against the cabin. "You stay there! Don't you move, Shiloh Coltrane, don't you move."

He did what she asked. If he could make her understand, soothe her distress, banish her mistrust, all would be well, for once and for all. Forever. He sat the horse like a statue, bone-tired as he was, and waited...

Until the scream pierced the air, birds flying off from branches, squawking on their way, and he galloped right up to the house as Sydney flew out.

"A snake, a rattler, on the edge of her cradle! Oh, lord, Shiloh, do something!" Sydney sobbed, folded over in her anguish.

He was in the house in two strides, and back out in as many, the snake held out between his two hands.

He laughed.

"Sweetheart, it's only an old bull snake. He's more

afraid of you than anything. Probably come in after mice or something." He tossed the snake away and headed back into the cabin for the crying baby.

"Look here," he whispered holding Meg to his chest and bouncing her a little. "Pappy's come home, darlin' precious. Look at you, sweet thing." He glanced at Sydney, tears streaming down her face, something between a smile and a frown masking whatever she felt. "Everything's gonna be fine now, little darlin'. Before you know it, you'll be riding round the ranch with Poppa and…"

Sydney came up to him, two damp spots blossoming on her shirtwaist. She held out her hands for the baby, and he eased the child across.

She sniffed as she settled onto a bench on the porch, opening her shirt to let the baby feed. "You look dreadful," she murmured.

"I know. I couldn't wait to see you a moment longer. Bones told me not to come 'til I'd bathed and all, but…" He was aware his own face was wet, tears running down as he watched the mother of his child let their baby suckle. He knelt in front of them and reached up to swipe away her tears, then brushed away his own. "Marry me," he whispered. "It was all I could think of, Syd, having a home with you, being a family, living on the ranch and having a good life. I know we will. Say yes, oh, please say yes?"

She slowly leaned across their baby as the crooked smile appeared on his worn face, barely visible through the growth of unkempt beard. With the lightest touch, she kissed his lips.

"Yes."

A word about the author...

A native New Yorker who has spent most of her life living in the U.K., Andrea Downing currently divides her time between the canyons of city streets and the wide-open spaces of Wyoming.

Her background in publishing and English Language teaching has transferred into fiction writing, and her love of horses, ranches, rodeo, and just about anything else western, is reflected in her award-winning historical and contemporary western romances. She has finaled twice for the RONE Awards, and won both the Golden Quill for Best Novella and the Maple Leaf Award for Favorite Hero, as well as several other honors.

You can find out more about her books at:
http://andreadowning.com/books

www.ingramcontent.com/pod-product-compliance
Lightning Source LLC
Chambersburg PA
CBHW070443260626
47161CB00004B/1185